W9-BKC-395

THOMAS MURPHY

THOMAS MURPHY

ROGER ROSENBLATT

An Imprint of HarperCollins*Publishers*

THOMAS MURPHY. Copyright © 2016 by Roger Rosenblatt. All rights reserved. Printed in the United States of America. No part of this book may be used or reproduced in any manner whatsoever without written permission except in the case of brief quotations embodied in critical articles and reviews. For information address Harper-Collins Publishers, 195 Broadway, New York, NY 10007.

HarperCollins books may be purchased for educational, business, or sales promotional use. For information please e-mail the Special Markets Department at SPsales@harpercollins.com.

FIRST EDITION

Designed by Suet Yee Chong

Library of Congress Cataloging-in-Publication Data has been applied for.

ISBN 978-0-06-239456-9

16 17 18 19 20   OV/RRD   10 9 8 7 6 5 4 3 2 1

For Alan and Arlene

THOMAS MURPHY

HAVE I TOLD YOU about this? The day they dropped the giant turf? It never happened, of course, but it was something. The sky was packed with balloonish clouds as dark as the turf itself. When we looked up, turf and sky were seamless, and it appeared that everything hanging over us, the entire universe, in fact, was turf. Only when the planes flew at a lower altitude of a few hundred feet could we distinguish the substance from the sky whence it descended. Even Mickey Kelleher, who was never impressed by anything, including The Great Houdini, had to admit it was worth looking at—the great brown grassy mass in the shape of a humongous brick, at least three and a half miles long and nearly as wide, suspended over the island and held in place by four hovering World War II B-24 Liberator bombers. The noise from the engines was dreadful. Thick wire cables extended from each of the huge planes to a sort of hammock on which the turf rested. At the scheduled moment, the planes would release the four cables, and the vast turf brick would drop on Inishmaan like a fallen star.

It was a gift from Dublin, we were told. Or was it Brazil? Sean Cafferty thought Korea, but Cafferty was always thinking that Aran and Korea had a mystical relationship. Whatever its provenance, the turf was supposed to have represented a generous gesture from the outside world to our people, a one-year supply of the most important thing in our lives. And it was true, at least from the viewpoint of us kids, that turf was the only thing the grown-ups ever talked about, when they weren't talking about dogs, pigs, horses, cows, and the size of Jocko Flaherty's head. And even when they were on other topics, turf always seeped into their conversations. So, naturally, everyone was excited as hell to look up at the big suspended beauty. The trouble was that the immense size of the thing, as long and wide as the island itself, made it impossible to find a place to stand where the turf would not drop straight on you.

So the entire population of the island, all 160 of us, including many of the dogs, pigs, horses, and cows, waded out to Galway Bay to the north, and into the Atlantic to the west, to watch for the big moment. Donkeys brayed. Babies murmured in their mothers' arms. As it happened, however, the turf was even bigger than we had estimated. When it finally dropped, as if from a massive celestial trapdoor, everyone on Inishmaan, and I mean every living thing—people, dogs, pigs, horses, and cows—were covered in the stuff. Turf filled our mouths, nostrils, ears, asses, and all the slots, holes, and openings of every man, woman, and beast. This took some getting used to, I don't mind telling you. But after a few minutes of standing there stunned, like pieces of sod ourselves, Casey Carey, I think it was, yelled, "Don't we smell good!" And the grown-ups looked around at one another and agreed. And instead of wailing and bemoaning the fact that everyone stank like shit, they carped the diem, and sang and danced and laughed, making a goddam festival of the moment. And no one took a bath for a week. Make that forever.

A POET I KNOW uses flammable ink. No sooner do his poems hit the paper than they burst into flame. How can one be consoled by your work? I asked him. You have to be quick, he said.

THE POINT IS (do you want a point?). The point is, you never crash if you go full tilt. Only the boyos whose feet tremble over the brakes veer off the road and go down in flames. Like those murders in the noir movies of the 1940s where some poor sap, doused in bourbon, is propped behind the steering wheel, with a cinder block laid on the accelerator, and the dark coupe, released toward the guardrail, flips headlights over taillights and slams into the cliff wall before plunging in the sea. You say that's different. That sucker was set up. But I say, no more so than the guy who drives his own car and slams on his own brakes just when he should gun it. Real fire comes from gunning it, with the curl of a grin on your ecstatic face, and the demarcations in the road shooting past, clickclickclick. The guardrail remains intact. Onlookers gasp, he'll kill himself at that speed. But you know better. You were never safer.

Only, who knows what it means to gun it at this age? And where to do the gunning? How to use the time. Understand? What, in the stages of final ambling, should be one's—what is the term—principal occupation? One's song. "What Are You Doing the Rest of Your Life?" That grand old courting tune. Do you know it?

Meanwhile, one by one, the loves of your life bite the dust through no fault of their own. Oona goes. Greenberg goes. In the white hospitals, in the green hospices, they stir from sleep and wanly smile or tell a joke or blow a kiss. Will I do likewise? Or, one blazing afternoon, on my seventy-third birthday, say, will I collapse in front of Rite Aid without ceremony, and lavish my attention on the sidewalk?

Bring it, Mr. Death, with your boney jaw and creepy cloak and outdated farming tools. Jeez. He looks like Wallace Stevens. Not that I don't love Wallace Stevens. What poet does not love Wallace Stevens. But that efficient look of his—the factual demeanor, competent eyes, combed-back white hair, not too long not too short, the jowls and fleshy cheeks, and the tweed sport coat, striped shirt, and black necktie, neat as a bird. A boyo you haven't seen since college, the class secretary who sang in an a cappella group and who now shills for the alumni association and sells insurance in Connecticut. Death. Am I right? Wallace Stevens with a scythe?

Oh, what the hell. Behold old Murph, anyway. The singing fool. Strong as a moth wing, a feather, a sheet of the thinnest vellum. I am resolute, needy, on my own, protected, protecting. Atomized. Unionized. A flivver, a toaster, a spore. So gorgeous I could drown in my reflection in the pool. So hideous I shrink from the bathroom mirror like a mollusk to its shell. I am like no one else, except that on occasion I resemble me—hysterical (both ways), Nazi, Jew, hit and miss, petal and ash. I celebrate myself and sing myself. I cannot bear myself, or my clumsy, inspired piano playing, or my scratchy, heavenly baritone belting out the great old tunes, or my sea-blue eyes, blameless as sunlight, guilty as sin. The creek and the stone and the tupelo tree. All that, and less, more or less. Give or take. Smart as a whip. Dumb as a post. Tumultuous, I sleep like a baby. Frail as pebbles.

IN THE HAYLOFT at Montgomery's barn, I fuck Cait. We are sixteen, and have just retreated from the pebbled beach at the cold edge of the ocean. Cait is not afraid of anything. She is beautiful in the way a red cart is beautiful, or rocks in a field. I do not love her, and she does not love me. But we've been companions since we were little, thrown together as kids are in the loneliness of the island, and now we've decided it's time to fuck. As for the Church, says Cait, the Church can go fuck *itself*. My kind of girl.

Around us in the hayloft lie things discarded by the Montgomerys that we brush aside to make room for our bodies—a handless alarm clock, picture magazines from Galway and Dublin, a locked steamer trunk bearing labels from Norway, Spain, and Turkey, a mirror in a rusted frame, a chalk drawing of the King of Somewhere seated on a tall throne with a yellow crown on his head and a scepter in his right hand.

We undress, Cait neatly arranging her skirt and sweater and underthings on a footstool, I tossing my stuff wherever. There's the narcotic smell of fresh paint from the main house, and the ever-present turf smoke rippling. We face each other on our knees. Cait takes my cock in her hands, and at once I grow hard. I reach between her legs. It takes a minute or so to get her wet. Then I am on top of her, about to brace my arms on either side of her shoulders, when my left hand comes down with all my weight on an inverted bottle cap that cuts deep in my palm. I glance at the blood, but am too worked up to stop. I fuck her and come right away. She lies there looking half asleep.

Her green eyes narrow as she gazes down her body at the trickle of blood on her thighs. She rolls away from me, and wipes off the blood with her hands. She dresses quickly. We do not speak. I have forgotten about my bloody palm until I snatch my clothing. Blood stains my skivvies, my shirt and socks. Cait laughs. You bleed too? she says. Well, I say, smiling at last, it is my first time.

SO NOW IT'S a thousand winters away from all that, and I'm sitting at my usual place in At Swim-Two-Birds, missing Oona, missing Greenberg, nursing four fingers of Jameson, and wondering how to weasel out of an appointment with the brain doctor my avid Máire has cornered me into—have I told you about this?—when a square-shouldered bruiser twice my size and half my age calls to me at the far end of the bar, and asks if I am who I am. I tell him I am, and ask if he knows me because he reads my poems. Never read a poem in my life, he says. Not even Yeets, he says (I didn't bother), and slides down to occupy the stool next to mine. No, he says. I recognized you from your picture in the papers last week, after you won some prize. You look older in person, he says. Just what I longed to hear. I figured you must be pretty good, he says. I could use a good poet.

That's a new one on me, I tell him. I never heard of anyone who could use a poet, good or bad. I can, he

says. I'm dying. Cancer of the colon. He pokes himself
in the belly. I learned the very day I saw your picture in
the papers, he says, so I thought it must be providence.
The doc says I've got three months at the outs. Sorry to
hear it, I tell him. But what does your dying have to do
with needing a poet? To help me tell my wife, he says. I
don't have the guts to do it myself. Or the brains, when
it comes to that. My wife is very sensitive, Mr. Murphy. A
flower, really. It takes a lighter hand than mine, he says.
I'm too ham-fisted. She needs to feel something more
than shock. She needs to feel how much I love her. I tell
him, You just said it all. No poet could put it better. Yeah,
he says. I'm good enough in a bar, with a couple of shots
in me, and talking to another guy. But with Sarah, I get
tongue-tied, especially in matters of the heart. Even after
eight years. I don't have the words, Mr. Murphy. I need a
poet. I need you.

I wished him well, but I had to say no. It didn't seem
right to speak to his wife about something that was per-
sonal business between the two of them. And, at any rate
I didn't want to involve myself in a stranger's life. But
you do it all the time, he says, looking more pained than
argumentative. He had a wide face and a ton of black hair,
thick as sedge, and the blue eyes of a child. How's that?
I say. He says, You ask the guy who delivers the grocer-
ies how he's doing. How's his family. His kids. You ask
the guy in the garage if his backache is better. See what I

mean? Everyone involves himself in some stranger's life, a little. It's normal. This would just mean doing it a bit more. And you wouldn't be involving yourself for more than an hour, Mr. Murphy. Add another hour to get to and from our place in Queens. Four stops on the F train. You'd go home with me. I'd introduce you to Sarah, and I'd leave the room. He considers. No, I'd stay with you. Yeah. That would be better. That way, I could hold her when she began to cry.

Look, I say. What's your name? John, he says. Everyone calls me Jack. Look, Jack. And everyone calls me Murph. Look, Jack. Can't you see that the matter of your dying is something that only you and Sarah ought to talk about? It's not for me to stick my nose in. This isn't like Cyrano de Bergerac. You know who that was? The guy with the nose? Your nose isn't all that big, he says, laughing, and thumps me on the back. Well, I say, what you're asking of me is much harder than someone voicing his passion for someone else. In a way, it's the same thing, he says. Only more urgent. Have another? Jimmy reaches across the bar and tops off my Jameson. You won't get me drunk to have your way with me, I tell my companion. He chuckles. Mud in your eye, he says. Listen to me, Jack. This may seem like a good idea right now, especially when you're upset, as you should be. But the matter of your dying is too intimate for anyone but the two of you.

The thing is, he says, I was hoping that a poet could

be intimate even if he doesn't know the person he's being intimate with, because that's what a poet does. Right? He's intimate without being intimate, if you see what I mean. I tell him he had something there, but my decision stood. It just didn't feel right. To be sure, the guy seemed sincere and smart and I liked what I saw of him. And he had a plight, I guess, apart from his dying, I mean. But Irish or not, I'm hardly the most gregarious fellow in the world, and anyway, I had things to do. All right, I didn't have things to do, except to try to avoid the brain doctor. I just didn't want to do this. Go home and tell your Sarah your own way, Jack. It'll be fine. He goes silent a moment. She's blind, he says. Sarah's blind. Then I go silent, too. Well—I turn to face him—she will be able to hear something more meaningful in your voice, the voice she loves, than in mine. I slide off the stool, shake his great hand, in which mine is lost, and say good night. Think about it, Murph? he says. I drain my glass. All right, I lie, and plough into the cold.

GET THIS, OONA. I'm in the Belnord elevator the other day with two assistant-vice-president-looking guys in their forties. One says to the other, I heard his mother died. The other says, yes, but she was ninety-four. Then they both nod like Chinese sages, as if the old dame's age made her death more acceptable. So, she was ninety-

four, I say to the assistant vice presidents. That makes
her death less noteworthy? Makes it okay? Because she
was an old bag? The two of them start to say something,
but I go on, calm as you please. An old bat? I say. A bat?
Maybe we can chop up her bat carcass, stick the pieces in
a grinder, and use her as bat guano, to fertilize your gardens, guys. Ninety-four! For Chrissake, you should have
bumped her off a long time ago, to decrease the surplus
population, as Scrooge said. You guys know Scrooge?
You should have knocked off the old crow with a Glock,
a Glock-knock, or stuck a shiv in her shriveled wrinkled
belly, or choked her till her bleary blue eyes popped out
of their sockets, like St. Lucy, or given her paper-thin
skin forty whacks with an axe, like Lizzie Borden. You
guys know Lucy? You guys know Lizzie? By now, my two
corporate buddies are backing themselves into a corner
of the elevator. But I'm on a roll. I sing it: Will you still
need me, or will you bleed me, when I'm ninety-four?
Nah. You guys had it right. When you gotta go, you gotta
go, but ninety-four is pushing it. Excessive. Over-the-
top. Tasteless. I for one am glad the wicked witch is dead.
Good riddance, I say. Tell you what. Let's the three of us
make a law—nobody lives past seventy-two. That way we
won't ever have to honor the aged, or waste our sorrow
or respect on some old broad who had the effrontery to
hang on. What do you say, guys? Deal? Would you believe
it, Oona? They looked at me like I was nuts.

LILLIAN HELLMAN was at a literary do I got asked to when I was a starting-out poet in New York. I overheard her tell some other big shot, "A crazy person is crazy all the time." Words of wisdom, in my young experience. Everyone on Inishmaan was crazy as a loon, myself not excluded, and that was true, perhaps especially, of the times they seemed stable. It helped to remember when you were holding a normal conversation with Big Head Flaherty, for instance, that normality was an anomaly, a break in Flaherty's regular weather, and that this was the same guy who shot his cow because, as Flaherty explained it, the cow had made a joke about the size of his head. I started to tell Ms. Hellman that she should visit Inishmaan to prove her point in spades. But I didn't have the nerve to interrupt her, as she was chatting away with John Berryman, who looked okay to me.

I WASN'T CRAZY. I just wanted to be alone, which may have seemed crazy on an island where most everyone was alone already, and that itself was alone. In school I failed every subject except solitude. Straight As in solitude. Since my school provided no teacher for that course, I had to award the grades to myself. I wrote no papers or exams, but I created some oral myths involving monks, tigers, lilac milk, and a magical three-legged stool. And another whopper about a day they dropped a giant turf on the island. All my stories were well thought of in my set, if I say so myself. Of course, I was the only person in my set, which necessitated my saying everything myself. I was a good listener, though. At night (most of the solitude classes were taught in night school), I would go down to the beach and listen to the shifts of the tides. Then I would rhyme the stars. Stars rhyme, if you give them half a chance.

One day, I took a walk toward no destination. The Atlantic unraveled in welts in the just-risen sun, and gravel glittered in the road, on which there was no one but nine-year-old me. I kept walking, past rain pools and speckled birds and flimsy weeds, blowing slightly. Everything was still. My breath was still. At a peak in the road, I came upon a fox, bright red and alert, stopped in his tracks. I too stopped, twenty feet or so from the fox. The redness of his nose merged with the white fur around his mouth. The points of his ears were tan, his eyes black and steady. And there we stood for who knows how long. A minute? A year? Our face-off, begun in apprehension, settled into a kind of understanding upon which no other creature intruded—not the cows in the rocky fields below us, or the sheepdog on the threshold of Doyle's cottage, or the terns. I recall no thought, no decision. I cannot speak for the fox. Then, at what seemed an agreed-upon moment, we turned away from each other, each proceeding in the direction whence we'd come. I did not turn to look at him again. But that night, in my bed close to the turf fire, I dreamed of a red bruise disappearing into the hills, and the furnace of his tail.

OONA SPOKE OF CREMATION. She preferred it to rotting in the ground, she said. Many do. And you? she said. What will it be, Murph. Earth or flames? Flames, I said. Like you, I'd rather be ash than Donne's bracelet of bright hair about the bone. And besides, I said, cremation won't require much of a transition. You've already given me the fire, darlin'. You too, said my hot little number.

SINCE THERE WERE ONLY 160 people living on the island, I used to count them. Every month or so. I would walk from house to house, completing the job in a day, or sometimes in a morning, if no one had died or was born after I got past his house, or was missing at sea. I made my tally in a spiral notebook, recording the names of every islander as neatly as I could, and writing the first and last names of everyone, including those in the same family. I'm not sure why I undertook this project, but taking my little census gave me a feel for the whole island. I hated the place, but I didn't want to lose anything about it either.

Afterward I'd climb down the escarpment to the beach with my notebook, and read the list aloud to the

sea. Mary Albright, Peter Andrews, Peter Brody, Michael
Brophy, Irene Cassidy—in alphabetical order, for the sake
of equality. I did not want the sea to think I played favor-
ites. After a while, the sea shouted the names back to me,
though not alphabetically. And sometimes it would jumble
the letters, creating new words. Powers became Worpes.
Law became Wall. Figgis, Figs. And so forth. Like me, the
sea never omitted a name. It understood Inishmaan, yet I
could not tell if love or hate came with its understanding.
Or mere indifference, maybe, the worst of all attitudes. I
put my money on indifference.

NINETY-THREE. Eighty-six. Seventy-nine. Seventy-two.
Dr. Spector is about to form an expression. Sixty-four, I
say, to see if she will indicate alarm or mere clinical interest. Máire searches my eyes for mischief. She calls me
Holden Caulfield without the maturity. The doctor says,
Remember, Mr. Murphy, we are counting down from one
hundred by sevens. Oh, I forgot, I say. In that case, sixty-
five. Did you really forget, Mr. Murphy, she says, or are you
just messing with me? It is the first thing to come out of
her all morning that makes me like her. I forget, I say. She
says, You think this is all a joke, Mr. Murphy? It depends
what you mean by all, I say.

Were it not for the eggs, none of us would have to go
through this arithmetical dance. Have I told you about

this? I'd like to say it could have happened to anyone, that it was a natural mistake. I simply forgot about the buggers. So the water boiled and boiled and then evaporated and the flames shot out from under the burning pot, onto a nearby roll of Bounty paper towels, thence to a wooden cutting board, thence to the backsplash. If the heat had not set off the fire thing, whatever it's called, on the ceiling, the whole house might have gone up. The entire Belnord, once the largest apartment house in the world. Whoosh. Just like that. Not the flames I had in mind to go down in. Danny Perachik, the super, the super snitch, called Máire, and she called the doctor. Jesus. It mattered not to Máire that I responded quick as a cat, swept down the extinguisher, which I had always wanted to try out anyway, and ended the crisis with a flourish. It was the last straw, she said, referring to previous straws involving the house keys and the car keys, and that time at Hornby's swimming pool. I wasn't safe living alone, she said. Everyone lives alone, I said. She gave me that look.

Nonetheless, so far so good. I am able to count down from one hundred by sevens. Look at me! I know what year it is. I can spell *syntax*. And *recommend*. If they asked me, I could even recommend a syntax. I can sing "Happy Birthday to You" flawlessly, like an angel. I sing it twice, once to Máire, once to Dr. Spector. I know the three branches of government, though I don't much care for them. I prefer tree branches, except for the government branch where the judges perch. I'm gaga over those robes. I know where I live, at least most of the time. And don't bring up that business with Mrs. Livingston last Friday, because all the apartment doors on my floor look alike, and after some initial frustration with the lock, and Mrs. Livingston's expression of terror and surprise, everything was jake. And you can tell that whinging rat Perachik to stop running to my daughter every time I piss and miss the can.

But Dad, says Máire, you still must come back for more testing. No bullshit, please? She touches my shoulder. I am uncertain as to whether my morning's performance has won me anything but a temporary pardon. I'd call the governor if I could remember his name. I put my hand on hers in a gesture of reassurance. Who am I kidding?

In the too-bright waiting room rises a rack of pamphlets on assisted living. Who does not need assisted living, may I ask. If no one required assistance in living, writers would be out of business. Máire and I prolong our conversation with Dr. Spector, each saying things we do not mean. The doctor is cute in her white coat, with a face full of character, a noble face, also inquisitive, like Joanne Woodward in *They Might Be Giants*. I give her a wink. She smirks in mock disgust, and hands me a manila folder. This is a take-home test, Mr. Murphy. I tell her take-home tests are my favorite kind, 'cause you can look up the answers. She says that if I look up the answers for this one, I'll wind up behind the eight ball.

"I've read your poems," she says.

"So you're the one"—old writer's joke.

"They're difficult," she says. "Like you." I smile. She doesn't.

"But worth the effort?" I am coy as a girl.

"We'll see," she says.

Dr. Spector bids me, Be well, which I take as a command. I hug my fretful Máire good-bye, and head for home, where I go straight for the fridge and toss out the eggs.

CRAZY, OONA, but after one full year I still shout your name when I enter the house. Crazier, I poke my head into every room, including the bathrooms, just in case. Then, failing to rouse you, I settle in the kitchen. I used to lament that we had so many rooms, especially after Máire grew up and out, and there were just the two of us to rattle around the joint. Now, I'm glad it's as big as it is, so I can postpone my disappointment when I cannot find you. I don't mind being alone, Oona. I mind being alone without you.

So, here's what I do—not always, but once in a while. I create a conversation with the furniture we acquired together, all of it, every piece. And the prints and paintings on the walls, too, including the Raphael Soyer sketch of the old man, who suddenly looks like me, and the eighteenth-century map of Ireland I spilled coffee on, and the English tavern table we got for a song at that auction in the Bowery. Every chair, lamp, stool. Every picture—that photo of wrinkled old Auden you bought me for my thirty-sixth birthday, half a life ago, predicting that I would have even more wrinkles than Auden when I reached his age. As I go through the lot, I ask you if you remember when exactly it was that we acquired this object and that.

Naturally, you get everything right, each precise detail of time, day, and weather, and who was wearing what. And as you tell me about the pencil drawing of Synge that I found for us on Merrion Square in Dublin, that's sitting on my writing desk now, or the fake Bokhara rug we were suckered into buying from that shyster on Mott Street, I too start to recall all the relevant information. I relive us. The entire process takes about two hours—Jesus, Oona, we have so much stuff. And when I'm finally done, having covered every item, I'm usually pretty tired, so I head for bed. Our bed, darlin' girl, I save for last.

ON THE OTHER SIDE of the wall, in his bed, Flynn lies with his death throes. That's how it is on the island. You die in the house you were born in, and you live there in between. Flynn is eighty-eight, his weight down to ninety-six pounds. His eyes are tide pools, his feet like crabs flinching on the beach. There's no voice left in him. Cait and I play checkers in the kitchen. We are ten. Through the wall, we hear Flynn thrashing about in his sheets, like rustling paper, but do not look up from the checkerboard between us. Flynn's daughter, Cait's ma, sweeps the floor. She does not look up either. She knows from birth how it is.

We have forgotten how to be sad here. I think that may be the worst of it—to forget how to be sad, and how important was a life. Cait studies the checkers, then double jumps me, letting her arms fall at her side. She frowns in victory.

THIS PLACE. This time. This time of life. If autumn is fall, winter is fallen. Stone harvest. This wine. This judgment, and the absence of judgment, meeting somewhere in the middle and the do-si-doing around this and that. This folk dance. This allemande left and allemande right. This graceless body. These rocks. Stone harvest. This desire to know and not to know, to be right and nothing close to right, to think with one's senses, and not to think. This going back to Flynn's death, to Cait. This going back to horses in the rain. This wish to ride and not to ride, but rather to watch others and wish them well. To move noiselessly in a curragh. Then in a kayak. Stone harvest. To observe and be part of, too. This state of equilibrium, tottering—o my Wallenda—this state of calm, of knowing how to do something, at long last. This discovery of form, of place. And bang! The hammer on the nail. The cracked jug. The flatiron. This water trembling in a glass, still and not still. This red door in a rock wall. This resignation. This endurance. This graceless body. These fields and beehives and dogs and donkeys. *Dia dhuit, asal.* This dolmen opening to light. This desolation. This chisel. This mortise. This remembering and forgetting, and remembering again, and knowing without remembering exactly. This faith. This gratitude. Say grace. This chair. This pen. Stone harvest. This black and white season that dies and lives for all eternity. This time of life. This time. This place.

A WEEK PASSES before I hear from Jack of the bar again, this time by a note. He must have secured my address from barkeep Jimmy, who, unlike most of his profession, is as discreet as a parrot. But what the hell. I had not forgotten about Jack and his blind Sarah—I remember what I want to. I don't mean to sound unfeeling about Jack's story, but there was something darkly appealing about the idea of talking to a blind woman about her husband's impending doom. Whatever Jack imagined about the power of poetry, this certainly would be a test. Feeling neither way, should I do it or not, I simply wondered if I could pull it off.

Jack's note was one line: "Still thinking?" And a phone

number beneath it. But the envelope also included a snapshot of Sarah, taken, it appeared, at Christmastime. She was standing with a Christmas tree behind her, the glow of the lights competing unsuccessfully with the glow of the girl. Naturally, I looked first at her eyes, which were gray and did not seem blind but full of wit and knowing. Her hair was like straw in the rain. Her face, neck, and arms were pink and tan. Her body was on the small side, and classic, a Vespa. Male that I barely still am, of course I studied her breasts. The cleavage showed in the arc of the collar of her dress, which was the color of jade, a foggy green. Something ironic or scolding about the mouth, I thought, and the way she was standing. It was a "Don't take a picture of me" pose, at once pleased and annoyed. I could hear her say, "Jack! Cut it out," just before she turned away.

It was her smile that kept me staring. Poets have a hard time conveying the quality of smiles. Cleopatra? Helen? I don't know. That caption of the Charles Addams cartoon showing Leonardo instructing the girl, "All right now, a little smile." What came to mind in Sarah's smile was breakfast. She had a smile like breakfast, like the beginning of a day of bright thoughts. She was unable to see the brightness she projected, yet she was that brightness. Promise, I thought. And kindness. A repertoire of encouraging remarks.

And yet, lurking within all that, like a shadow on the moon, was a spot, a grove of disappointment, as though

the breakfast she had prepared with so much hope in it,
had gone cold. Or perhaps the one for whom she had prepared it had arrived late and caused it to go cold. Beauty.
I used to think it consisted of flowers and the arts. No
longer. The idea of beauty that grows in the mind as one
ages, and finally presents itself as a fact, has discarded all
former impressions and standards. Its eyes are tired now.
It wears a shawl. Its sun subdued. It is sadder than phlox
and angrier than Lear. The beauty of the lurid lights in the
hallway of an apartment building. Of a smudged forehead
on Ash Wednesday. The beauty of rocks in a field. You are
aware only of its denials. The other night I caught the face
of a bitter man on TV. I did not know the source, but it was
beautiful, his bitterness.

   I placed Sarah's photo on my writing desk, beside the
drawing of Synge. I don't know why. Now she did not seem
so alone.

ALONE. THE OTHER DAY the TV had a news story about an
outbreak of the Ebola virus in Nigeria and Sierra Leone.
The TV doctor made earnest reassurances that the pan-
demic will not come here. This isn't Africa, he said. But
where it is Africa, another doctor working with those who
have contracted the virus reported on what it's like to die
of the Ebola. The TV showed a man in an isolation ward,
disappeared into a head-to-toe white Hazmat suit, with

a chicken's-head cap and his eyes like dark stones in a whiteout. When you have the Ebola, said the doctor, you die alone. No family member can touch you. No one can touch you or be near you. Jeez. Living alone is one thing. But dying alone?

IF WE'RE TALKING DYING, you should have seen the way we did a funeral on Inishmaan. When anyone checked out, the family placed the coffin in front of the cottage door, and women from all over the island would come and keen and beat the boards of the coffin with their fists. After that, the men would tie ropes around the coffin, and take it by cart to the graveyard that sloped to the sea. Then the family grave was opened—there was one grave per family—and the blackened boards and the bones of the previous tenant were removed to make room for the new one. Sometimes the skull of an old family member would be propped up on a gravestone. I saw Mrs. Fallon take her mother's skull, toss it in the air, laugh like a hyena, and carry it back to her house. The men would measure the length and breadth of the new coffin with switches cut from brambles near the road. When the coffin was ready to be lowered into the grave, the women came to it again, like hungry birds, and keened and beat it with their fists, more fiercely than before. The grave was filled with dirt, and the islanders returned to their lives.

SAYS HERE, in this article on biology and aging (whoever thought I'd be reading this stuff?), that nature doesn't give a shit about the parts of our makeup that deal with thinking and reading and feeling and love. Or, it gives a shit, but only for a time. The repository for those functions is our somatic cells, which serve as mere protectors, bodyguards, to the germline DNA. The somatic cells of each generation become irrelevant genetically once the germline DNA goes about its re-creating business. Somatic cells are destroyed at the end of every generation and have to be regenerated, or created whole cloth with every baby born. In other words, if I understand this aright, those activities we prize for making us most human do not count in the species' pursuit of itself.

No surprise, when you think about it. Flynn dies. Oona dies. Greenberg dies, though not because of his DNA. Maybe because of the DNA of the man who killed him. I, in stark contrast, live. So do Máire and Dr. Spector. So do Jack and Sarah and Jimmy, the bartender. And the creep, Perachik. He lives. Can't say selection isn't random.

And I'm not sure about this anyway. I mean, if love and feeling need to be re-created with each generation, with no DNA to carry their somatic cells forward, why do children seem to love their parents right off, soon as they pop out? Suckling? Not all kids suckle, but they seem to be born cooing and gooing toward ma and da. My grandson William loves me and I love him, and that's the way it's been with us since our eyes first locked. Can't tell me that we learned to love each other, that we calculated the academic subject of each other and then arrived at an informed decision. We just loved. Like that. Like his mother with Oona and me, and us with her. We just did it. I don't know. Maybe it's the pure biology of need. But it seems more intuitive, uh, natural than that to me. As I said, what do I know?

On the other hand, what's so bad about each generation having to drum up its own inclinations for thinking and reading and feeling and love? Its own love songs. Every generation has its own love songs. You can say that nature's relegation of such features to mere guardian status shows how little it cares for those features. But, in a poetic sense, the only sense I have, the fact that our humanness has to be born again and again, may test the worth of the race far more severely than seeing whether or not we can grow to fight off some germs. Maybe nature is showing exactly how much it values us by requiring our artistic and spiritual regeneration. Tests how durable we are in terms of creativity. Oh, nature. You sly devil. The Romantics went all jelly-kneed thinking that babies were originally born in heaven, and they may have dreamed up this notion because they could not abide the idea that people have to start life anew, every human for himself. I, for one, love that idea. It makes each of us a god of our own creation. Including Danny Perachik. Did I say that?

TO THINK OF IT! A pip-squeak like Perachik, with the brain of a dead mole, in charge of a gem like the Belnord! The Belnord! The Beautiful North. Belle of the North. An old beauty, like meself. Windows wide as a man's wing-span. Italianate arches. Limestone walls. I grew up with limestone, and now I live in it. The vast front hall of our apartment. Four enormous bedrooms. Four bathrooms with little octagonal white tiles on the floors. A bathroom for the two maids' rooms (not that we had a single maid, or even a part-time cleaning lady, since you can guess what Oona said about the necessity of that). Parquet floors everywhere. Black and white squares for the kitchen lino-leum. The floor space of the kitchen itself, larger than my childhood cottage. Closets you could not just walk in. You could ride your trike in 'em, like Máire. Twelve-foot ceil-ings, with wavy plaster designs near the top. And all this magnificence for a rent that's stabilized, unlike meself.

Up goes the building in 1909, a full square block reaching from Amsterdam to Broadway, and from Eighty-sixth to Eighty-seventh. Twelve stories of apartments as big as my own in a blockade surrounding a courtyard, with landscaped gardens and pathways leading to the entries and a fountain in the center like an open rhodo-dendron. There I am. See? On a stone bench, and Máire on her trike, taking the pathways in her giggly zoom. And beneath that courtyard, at the basement level, yet another courtyard the same size, where horse-drawn wagons deliver milk and ice, and where the superrich residents, lured by architectural elegance from downtown to the northwest prairie, keep their own horses. Soon Isaac Bashevis Singer will be in residence here. And Zero Mostel. And Marilyn Monroe, would you believe it. Not to mention, the incomparable, unflappable, unforgettable, unstoppable poet of the age, Sir Thomas James Murphy, Esq. himself. OBE, QED, LBJ, TNT.

In 1909 they're soldering the bolts of *Titanic* in Belfast (it was okay when it left here—old Irish joke). And Babe Ruth is testing his teenage pitching arm, and the Archduke Ferdinand is not archduking it out with anyone yet and Tsar Nicholas is still tsaring in his own show. Shackleton is shackled to the South Pole, as Admiral Peary veers toward the North. Baby Simone Weil arrives, as do babies Isaiah Berlin and Max Baer and James Mason and Gene Krupa and Eudora Welty. Someone is singing "Shine On, Harvest Moon" for the first time. Can you hear her?

Come to the window. There's Paul Robeson, age eleven, walking hand in hand with his ma. He looks up in wonder. Do you know what that is? his mother asks him. The boy shakes his head. That's the *Belnord*, Paul. That's the *Belnord*!

THAT'S BOTSFORD. He parks his Vespa near the fountain in the courtyard, where the chrome catches the lights of the building and the blue chassis gleams like the blue eye of the *vampyroteuthis infernalis*, the vampire squid from hell. The great globular eye staring at you, taking you in, sizing you up. The Vespa is that eye, blue eye, the blue with a light in it. I stop and walk around it. And again. Most every night. The tan leather seat, a saddle for a show horse. I know where Botsford keeps the key in the building office, know exactly where it hangs on a hook. Never rode one of these babies. Never took one of these bad boys out for a spin. You know what they say. If you put a loaded Vespa in a play, eventually someone is going to have to ride it. That's what they say.

DEAR MURPH,

It occurs to me—your brooding mind being what it is—that you may think I'm trying to lock you up in the loony bin. I'm not. You probably ought to be locked up in the loony bin, but that condition long preceded your recent shenanigans. I'm concerned that you'll harm yourself. It's that simple.

Your dutiful and loving daughter,
Máire

Dear Dutiful and Loving,

I'm sorry, but I never had a daughter, and I don't know anyone named Máire. My friend Greenberg

used to sing about a table down at Morey's. Is that
you? Or are you the old gray *mare*, who ain't what she
used to be? Ah, but who is?

Dear Murph,
    Go fuck yourself.

Dear Máire,
    Oh! Now I remember you.

MY DRINKING BUDDY sits beside me on the couch. She
has milk, I have coffee. She writes too, with a purple
crayon and a legal pad half her size. Every so often, she
glances up at me, as if to check that we're both on course. I
look back at her and nod. Her legs stretch not quite to the
rug. We continue this way, in silence, writer and writer.
Oona sneaks us a look and smiles.

Something telling about my drinking buddy from the
start. Self-confidence absent of self-interest. I am driving her and four other little girls home from a birthday
party. They sit in the back. One of the girls gets carsick,
and heaves. Three of the others back away, with *eww*s and
*gross*es. Only my drinking buddy goes to comfort the girl.
She holds her hand and wipes her mouth and the front of
her dress.

My drinking buddy and I dine out in a fancy restau-

rant, just us two. Oona stays home. She wants us to have
a special evening. My drinking buddy dresses in a white
blouse, a little green tunic, high white socks, and Mary
Janes. She prances into the restaurant, like a rich girl, but
without the hauteur. Part sashay, part swagger. No sooner
have we been guided to our table than she announces she
has to go to the ladies' room. She walks off, returning
shortly. A minute or so later, she goes to the ladies' room
again. Returns. Sits. Then she has to go again. I ask her
if she's sick. No, she says, I just like going to the ladies'
room.

My drinking buddy wants to change her name. None
of her fellow second graders can pronounce it. They'll
learn, I say. That accent mark, she says. They don't get it.
They'll learn, I say. Even my teacher, Mrs. Rosario, can't
pronounce it. She'll learn, I say. It's an ancient Irish name,
I tell her. Máire. It goes back to the Norman invasion. The
normal invasion? Norman, I say. Norman who? she says.
Daad! I want a regular girl's name, like Tiffany or Skye.
Tell you what, I say. We'll call you Ralph. Good, she says,
hands on hips. I'm Ralph.

A framed photo of my drinking buddy riding a camel
in Jerusalem stands on the piano. Beside it, a photo of
her in a Sailfish. Beside that, one at her graduation from
Brown, the mortarboard deliberately cockeyed on her
head. Beside that, her holding just-born William.

Before that, she is in business school at NYU, and she

comes over late at night, and sits beside me on the couch. Oona is long asleep, so it's just us two. We listen to the old songs, the standards, on the radio. Mr. Jameson joins us. My drinking buddy always has taken to whiskey, a genetic inheritance, and can drink her old man under the table, though she rarely tries. We sit and chat and sing in thirds harmonies—"If you're ever in a jam, here I am." Sometimes I'm writing, and sometimes she has homework. She looks across at me every so often, for old times' sake. *Mon semblable. Mon scold.*

WHEN SAINT JOHN JAMESON established the Bow Street Distillery in Dublin, in 1780, what tests did he devise for the whiskey to see if it was good? I wonder. Body? Color? Did he work out the balance between malted and unmalted barley, and dry the liquid in a kiln to achieve just enough sweetness on the tongue and burn on the throat? Or did he use a different sort of test entirely, one that led to one million gallons of Jameson produced every year? Did he say to himself, if this makes grief go away, it's a keeper?

ONE FOR THE ROADS? All Inishmaan roads are divided in three parts: the stone walls on either side, the two tracks for carts and cars, and the island of tall grass and flowering weeds between the tracks. Of these three, only one is connected with motion or travel. The island and the walls represent the stationary. In every road, therefore, lies the dual possibilities of Ireland. Stay or go. But the road remains the same, giving of nothing, no hint as to which way of life it tends or recommends. Like certain poems.

You can thus read into each road a lesson in freedom of choice. I made no such reading. I knew I would go eventually, and I saw the roads only as statements of clean clarity, nouns, beautiful for what they were, and not for the ways they might relate to me. The same was true of the trees on Inishmaan and the gaggles of wildflowers and the houses and the pubs and the pigs in their folklore. Each life unto itself in this stupefying world.

INTO THE SAME NIGHT I walk as I did as a child, welcoming the same defeats, desires, usurpations. This irrevocable pilgrimage. As one says after a good conversation with a friend, where did the time go? Emerging from At Swim-Two-Birds, I battle a snootful. Grim kids swagger on Eighty-seventh and Columbus. A wintry creature, his keen animal's face shining in the hoarfrost, takes command of the curb. I know him from the church shelter where I teach a poetry workshop to my homeless beauties once a month. Murph! he cries. Arthur! I cry. He is huge, made of heavy curves and rounded edges. Arthur the Bear! Nobody knows if he's black or white, his skin is so caked with soot. Murph the Bard! He's in a good mood tonight. You can tell when he's not. Dr. Reynolds, the minister at the shelter, the only clergyman I've ever known with a sense of humor, calls Arthur a bi-polar bear. Murph! Arthur and I greet each other as if at sea.

All is in decline. Empires, literacy, gaudy birds. I follow a trail of rotting flowers from the Koreans' convenience store to a snowy ravine where ice has seized the upper boughs. My teeth clench. One of these days I'm going to learn to hold my liquor. One of these days I'm going to learn to hold my recriminations. S'long, Murph! See you, Arthur! Show me the way to go home.

Why did I not write Snodgrass? It was 1975, and he'd liked a poem of mine in the *Antioch Review.* I cannot recall why I did not write him back. Snodgrass. Poet of "Heart's Needle" and "April Inventory." Poet of quiet dread and silver maples. I have come to a stage of recriminations when one wonders not why one did certain things in a life, but rather why not. And all the things not done are almost always the easy things, requiring the least amount of effort. Life defined by the loss of casual opportunities. Small beer. Why did I not write Snodgrass? To thank him. To gush. To tell him, if only some day, one day, even if by dumb luck, I could write a line like "my lady's brushing in sunlight," well I'd die happy. We had a friendship in the offing. I offed it. I was stunned. Was that it? I was scared. Was that it? I was a cocky bastard, thinking, *of course* he

likes my work. Why *shouldn't* he? We're *equals,* Snodgrass
and I. Two peas in a poem. Was that it? Why did I not write
Snodgrass?

TO WALK THROUGH the landscape of a life. Odd, the
scenes and moments that elbow their way to positions of
prominence. The dear, quiet morning in the field with my
ma, when she was naming a flower. The student at Mary-
mount, the ecology zealot. Such a mouth on her, but oh,
could she write. A broom leaning in the corner of the cottage. A saw's wheezing through a plank of pine. A chas-
tised dog. Cait's freckled thighs. The blunt smell of dung
and oil lamps. Soggy biscuits on a yellow plate. The time
in Long Island Sound when Oona learns to swim. You go,
girl. A sky slumps, defeated. Trout in flight. The wing of
a silver seaplane, tipping toward the horizon. Ella on the
radio. "Come Rain or Come Shine." So perfect was her
pitch, the members of the band tuned their instruments
to her voice. A plough making a circle as it passes over a
field. A cloud of lambs. The poise of an egret. The bent
teeth of a harrow. The brainstorm. The fury. The pudgy
school friend of Máire who asked what a poet does, and
when I told him, he laughed. *Ubi sunt, ubi sunt.* The rocks of
Inishmaan. The pigs of Inishmaan. The mud. The mud of
Inishmaan, thick, dark, descending in layers to the center
of the Earth. A hearse drawn by a farm horse, the wood

painted red and black. Oona answers the priest, I do—
mostly. Greenberg hoists us in a chair. An aged woman at
an outdoor reading smiles and nods at every right word,
the grass trembling at her feet. Her eyes, bright gray.
Snodgrass. Where did the time go?

OVER THE ROCK FIELDS I climbed to Synge's Chair—that
formation of rocks shaped like a caveman's throne, where
J. M. Synge is said to have brooded his plays and essays
into being. Synge's Chair. Have I told you about this?
That great granite head of his, and the iron mustache. I
would trudge to Synge's Chair, yearn toward the Atlantic,
remain till nightfall, and mark the red declension of the
sun. Then I'd return home and my da would read to me
in my bed. My unshaven, baritone da of the red creased
neck and the whiskey breath. He would prop his one existing leg on the low stool in front of the fire, and read me
Padraic Colum and James Stephens, and sometimes even
Kavanagh, when da was in his cups.

His favorite was Yeats. He'd read me the early poems,
easier for a boy to understand, such as "At Galway Races,"
"These Are the Clouds," and "Brown Penny." He loved
"Brown Penny"—a young man's poem, he said—and he
recited it from memory. Lusty, wistful, plain sad sometimes, as he'd glance at his left leg, then at the space where
his right leg used to be. He'd lost that one in a thresher,

when he was eighteen. He never complained, never a word, just that glance at the absent leg. More than the books, that taught me how to write a poem.

They really aren't difficult, my poems, no matter what the good Dr. Spector says. Greenberg got 'em readily enough. Oh, I'll toss in a wild word from time to time, to keep the reader on his toes, the way Heaney does, and Paul Muldoon. But neither of those great fellas is hard to understand, and I'm not either. Most of the poets of my race are not hard to understand. We just play hard to get.

Basically, we're piano bar players, singing our guts out and writing by ear. Which is probably why the ancient Irish poets were known in their kingdoms as The Music. Poets were called The Music. When the kings did battle with one another, which was every other day, they dispatched their soldiers with orders to kill everyone in the enemy camp, every man, woman, and child, including the opposing king. Kill 'em all, said the king. Except The Music. The soldiers were forbidden ever to kill The Music. Because he was The Music.

A POEM SHOULD consist of two parts rocks, one part daisy. 'Tis my opinion, anyway. If the rocks aren't in the poem, you won't be able to appreciate the daisy. And if you take out the rocks, so all that's left is daisy, well, that's all that's left. It's not so yellow anymore. It wilts. You want hard language to convey soft thought, because in the end all poetry is about love, and no one wants love without a backbone. It's about contrast, see. The kiss and the slap. Oona and I never fucked so brilliantly as when we'd gone at each other beforehand, really torn each other up, tooth and claw. Then we'd hurl ourselves into bed and make a poem.

Live like a bourgeois and think like a god.

—Flaubert, in Thomas Murphy's *Book of Dandy Quotations*

AND WHAT DO YOU suppose that means? I ask my homeless beauties as we sit around two card tables pressed together in the rec room of the church. " 'Live like a bourgeois and think like a god.' " What's a bourgeois? says Malik, a man of indeterminable age, with a mound of brown hair piled on his head, and wearing a blue scarf like a blanket. He looks like hell. They all look like hell in the shelter, which accounts for their loveliness. A bourgeois, an ordinary person, I tell him. A shopkeeper. You call that ordinary? says Malik. If I had a shop, I'd be a king. The four others nod, all except Arthur, who moves to a different drummer. His actions are slow and definite, unconnected to anything in the conversation. He seems in a dark mood today.

If I had a shop, says Katie, I'd sell blouses. Katie's in her fifties, I think, and dresses only in white—white sweater, white slacks, white shoes. If I had a shop, says Florence, I'd sell myself. Everyone laughs. Were floozies still in sway, Florence would be their queen. We're off the subject, I tell them. What does it mean to live like a shop-keeper, like a regular Joe, and think like a god? It means, says Alexander, as if drawing on a pipe, that one must dream above one's station. Alexander was once a private secretary to a billionaire. He is tall, reed thin, and south-ern. He went to Princeton, and speaks of stations. Station? says Florence. I lived in Grand Central two years, and I'll tell you, it was hard to live above it. Look, I say, sorry I brought up Flaubert in the first place. It's always a bad idea to begin a class with a Frog. Look, Alexander is right, mostly, I tell them. The idea is to live a simple life, which is constricted and has boundaries, but to dream without limits, to have that power. Like a god, says Malik. Like a god, I repeat. Yes, Malik.

What does that have to do with writing poems, Murph? asks Florence. You tell me, my beauty. She brightens when I call her that, and gives me a smile and a wink. It means, says Alexander, that we must be clear and simple in the way we write our poems, but soar to the heavens in our subjects. Very good, Alexander, I tell him. He never reacts to compliments. Doubtless, the bil-lionaire hired him for his discretion and decorum. We must write in a way that people understand our poems, I say. Calmly and quietly. But what we write about can and should take off like a rocket.

In fact, they all are quite good poets, naturals. Nearly every client in the shelter is schizophrenic, which means they have trouble making narrative connections. What's anathema for normal social life is meat for the poet. The poet doesn't want to make connections. He leaves that to others. Mustn't congratulate them on their illnesses, however. Somewhere in the holy messes of their minds, they would prefer to be pain free, not poets.

We pass around the poems they've done in the month since our last meeting. Katie has written a haiku. "She loves to wear white./ Daddy will be in her room./ White is her color." Do you want to talk about your poem, Katie? I ask. She keeps her head down. You never know how far to go with them. At the same time, you want to get even the worst things out on the table. Is this about sex abuse? I ask her. Sure it is, says Florence. Katie keeps still. Well (I gulp), let's look at what Katie has given us as a poem, not as something that happened. Happens to everyone, says Florence. But see how Katie has written it, I say. Why does she write "Daddy," and not "My father"? Too many syllables for the haiku, says Alexander, looking smug. To show she loves him anyway, says Florence. And what does Daddy do with her love? I ask. Crushes it, says Malik. Rapes it, whispers Katie. Yes, Katie, I reach across the table and touch her white sleeve. And this is terrible, the worst thing. But, darlin', see what you have done with this terrible thing. You have made it into a work of art. She keeps her head down still. This is what we sometimes do as poets, you see? I tell them, taking the spotlight off Katie. We say to our readers, this is how bad life can be. But this is also how gorgeous we can make it, by way of art. Do my beauties understand? I'm not sure.

Arthur has written a poem consisting of one line. What's it called, Arthur? "Black," he says. It's called "Black." Will you read it to us, Arthur? His voice rises from a well. "My cave is black," he says. Is that the whole deal? says Malik. Arthur says nothing. His mind is elsewhere. Inadequate, says Alexander. Woefully inadequate. I like it, says Katie. Me too, says Florence. It's direct. It says all that Arthur wants to say about his cave. Good, Florence, I say. When Arthur is not staying at the shelter, he lives in a cavelike arrangement of boulders near Wollman rink in the park, an oversize version of Synge's Chair. He calls it his summer place. I start to say a few encouraging words about his poem, but he cuts me off. Murph! he shouts exuberantly, as if aware of my presence for the first time. Murph the Bard! Arthur the Bear! I say. He turns away.

I'M HERE to pick up my best friend.

It figures that your best friend is a four-year-old, says

Máire. She calls, William? Your best friend is here to go for a walk with you. Máire and William live one block east of the Belnord, on Eighty-sixth between Columbus and Amsterdam. Makes it easier for her to get to me, and Perachik to her.

Out trots William from the back of my daughter's apartment. Red T-shirt. Red sneakers. Red puffy winter jacket. Whenever I ask him his favorite color, he says blue. Big smile on him. Big smile on me. I have a picture of myself on Inishmaan at his age. Same hair, same eyes.

It's not a walk we're going on, is it, William? Tell Mommy. It's an adventure! he says. Máire zips up his little jacket. Don't let him out of your sight, she says.

I won't, I assure her.

I was talking to William, she says.

If you're wondering why Máire has no husband, she did have one, a prick named Hughie to whom she gave the boot when he was caught canoodling with a fellow real estate crook just about the time William was born. There was nothing noteworthy about Hughie except his name, which invited "fuck" preceding it. William inquires of him from time to time, as he would about a toy he barely remembers.

Central Park, William! I swing my arm in an expansive gesture. Isn't it grand? A spot of green within the Black Forest! He never has to understand what I'm talking about to know what I mean. His hand slips into mine as we cross

Central Park West to begin our sojourn. William takes in everything, as if he were poring over an ancient text. His expression, when not laughing, is scholarly, monastic. Where should we go today, William? I ask him.

To the Land of the Flying Donkeys, he says, referring to the subject of our last get-together. Why do donkeys fly, Murph?

Why do donkeys fly, William? Who said they don't?

I said they do, Murph. Donkeys fly.

Oh. Why didn't you say so? Why do donkeys fly? You might as well ask me why donkeys fly!

He giggles. You're silly, Murph.

I'm silly? *You're* silly. You're the silliest person I've known since Elephantus.

Who is Elephantus, Murph?

Who is *Elephantus*? You might as well ask me, who is Elephantus! All right, I'll tell you. He was King of the Elephants.

Was he very big?

That's just the thing, William. He was as small as you. And that is why the elephants made him their king. He was unusual.

Is it good to be unusual? he asks. We are making our way east through the park.

Yes. It's great to be unusual.

You're unusual, Murph. You're the most unusual person I know.

We approach the bronze statue of Balto, the Siberian husky. I point it out. Well, that's the most unusual person *I* know, William.

That's not a person, Murph. That's a dog!

That's a person, William. Wouldn't you say he's unusual? He roars. We sit on a bench. There follows the rapid gunfire of typical William questions. If zebra stripes are brown, why do they look black? When do caterpillars realize they want to become butterflies? Do horses know that they're racing? How many rabbits would it take to push over the Empire State Building? Are you going to die, Murph?

What? I look concerned. He looks matter-of-fact.

Are you going to die?

Everything dies, William. But I plan to be around for at least another hundred years. He gives me a hug. We circle the Reservoir, then walk to the carousel, shut down for winter. He climbs up on a stationary horse. You've read a lot, haven't you, Murph?

I have. And you will, too, when you get the knack of it. I mount the horse behind him. He's just learning to read now. He loves *Harold and the Purple Crayon,* and hates all of Dr. Seuss, as do I.

Who read to you when you were little, Murph?

My da. Want to get ice cream? We head in that direction.

What did he look like, your da?

Like me. Only he had a nose as long as a fire hose. He laughs.

You have a nose as long as an anteater's, he says.

You have a nose as long as Elephantus. In fact, it's so long, it's dragging on the ground.

You have a nose as long as a fart. He screams with laughter at his own joke.

Mommy would not approve of your saying *fart,* William. I keep a straight face.

You just said it yourself, Murph! You always say it.

Fart? (Shocked and dismayed.) Fart? Why, William, I have never said *fart* in my life. He gives a sly smile as we bounce along, arriving finally at the ice cream wagon. What flavor will it be, William? Chocolate?

Fart, he says.

They don't have that flavor, I tell him.

He looks resigned. Chocolate, then, Murph. He thanks me and takes the cone. We sit together on a bench.

William—in my most severe, grown-up, authoritative voice—we must agree never to say *fart* again.

He nods gravely, until a moment passes and we shout in unison, Poop!

WILLIAM AND I occupy the world's not, a phrase I picked up in E. R. Dodds's *The Greeks and the Irrational,* the sort of book I've been drawn to lately. In it Professor Dodds writes of Dionysus, the Master of Illusions, who could make a vine grow out of the plank of a ship, and allow his votaries "to see the world as the world's not." The world's not. Such a phrase. To be differentiated from the world's is, I suppose.

According to Dodds, the Greeks saw the gods as jealous and interfering, resentful of the successes and happiness achieved by mortals, which might hoist our mortality above its proper station. The gods did not want us to be gods, or to be happy. Even heroism did not breed happiness. In *The Iliad*, the sole reward for heroes is fame, not happiness. And people, helpless, feared their gods as agents of approaching doom. The powerful Apollo promised security to the humble. Understand your station as a man, he said in *The Iliad*. "Do as the Father tells you, and you will be safe tomorrow."

But Dionysus, bless him, had a different view, and a different power. He offered freedom. He was essentially the god of freedom, a singer of love songs, says Dodds, who was an Irishman, of course. Better educated, but we're all the same bastards. Small wonder the professor took up this project in the first place. Who but my fellow mick would be drawn to the Master of Illusions? Not to mention the matters of trances, magic, and madness. Dionysus said, forget the distance between gods and men, and don't concern yourself with safety. You never crash if you go full tilt. Be happy today, he said. He was a god of joy, and also of democracy, which was deemed accessible to all. I'm sure I met him in the pubs in Inishmaan. Big lumbering boyo. Farmer's hands, a roar of a laugh. The advocate of laughter. He didn't want us to be and stay mortal. He wanted to live like a bourgeois and think like a god.

Hard to say what to make of all this. But I am growing a deep affection for Dodds, and for Dionysus. They become the gods of ecstasy, out of this stasis, deities of the world's not. I've always been a bad Catholic. I've worked hard at being a bad Catholic, and I don't mean lapsed. The eunuch priest from the mainland. (We were grateful he was a eunuch.) The keening, the screaming statues, beads bleeding in your hands. The cows of heaven await you, children. The heart's cross. I have faith in that.

But I could be a good Dionysian. To the altar of that god I'd go daily, devout as my ma. I'd take the body and blood of Dionysus in one gulp. And I'd pray the Lord's Prayer to Dionysus: Our Father, who art in heaven, let me out.

AS IF TO REMIND ME that I'm not out yet, or likely to get there, Dr. Spector calls to inquire if I've finished the take-home yet. I ask her if she knows anyone I can copy the answers off. Planet Earth, Mr. Murphy, she says. Where's that? I say.

THOMAS MURPHY ON COOKING
FOR ONESELF

Hamburgers and steaks are fairly easy. Just plop 'em in
the frying pan and see what happens. Eggs can be trouble. I'd stay away from eggs, unless you scramble them,
because you have to keep your eye on scrambled eggs all
the time, unlike hard-boiled eggs, which one may forget
to watch, and then they bite you in the ass. Cold cereal is
good. Special K is an old standby, but I also am develop-
ing a fondness for Cinnamon Toast Crunch. Speaking of
which, cinnamon toast is no trouble either, if you pur-
chase a container of cinnamon and sugar already mixed.
I don't eat cinnamon toast myself, but I make it for William when he visits. Zone bars too are easy. Just unwrap
and eat. Also, fruit, as long as it isn't a pineapple that
requires carving up. Here's a nice surprise: jellied cran-
berry sauce is tasty straight out of the can. Of course,
the best way to go for most meals is takeout. No muss,
no fuss. In the Belnord area, there's takeout for Chinese,
Japanese, Thai, Ethiopian, Indian, Cuban, and pizza at
a place where you can get meatball subs as well. A few
months ago, I got a call from an editor who was compil-
ing a book of writers' favorite recipes. I sent him seven
phone numbers.

THOMAS MURPHY ON CLEANING AND WASHING
FOR ONESELF

Dry-cleaning is a bloody cinch, as long as you know
which of your clothes requires it. For dry-cleaning,
just take the appropriate clothing to the dry cleaner.
The one on Eighty-seventh and Columbus is reliable,
and the people are pleasant. Dry-cleaning is opposed
to wet cleaning, which you can do yourself in a washing
machine, followed by a dryer. (You can distinguish the
washer from the dryer by the large cylinder in the center of the former.) After Oona, when I had to do all the
washing myself, I found I was pretty able with a washing
machine. Once in a while, I toss in too much liquid Tide,
which adds a stickiness to the clothing, and occasionally I forget the Bounce, but it doesn't seem to matter.
In the beginning, I had a little trouble doing the sheets
and towels because I didn't know how long it took to dry
them. But I'm okay now, especially with pj's, skivvies,
T-shirts, and socks. I make a mistake from time to time
and include a dress shirt with the wash, giving the shirt
that wrinkled look the Gap creates deliberately. No big-
gie, as the kids say. I've had only one real mishap, but
I learned from experience. Last summer I bought a suit
that said Wash 'n' Dry on the label. I figured that meant it
did not need dry-cleaning, and I further surmised that I
could save a step in the washing process by wearing the

suit in the shower, and soaping myself up and rinsing off. I used Oona's hair dryer after that, but the suit was still damp when I wore it out on the street. I won't do that again. Live and learn.

THOMAS MURPHY ON DREAMING FOR ONESELF AND OTHERS

Dream up, not down. Up. Tyrants dream down, businessmen dream laterally, poets dream up. That's how you can remember it. Dream up.

DREAM WAY UP, especially on a day when Moses comes walking and talking on Seventy-ninth Street. When something like this happens, I don't know about you, but I listen. Prophets like Moses don't come along every day, after all, and they don't grow on trees, though that would be fun to picture. The old guy shows up every five thousand years or so, that's about it, and he doesn't dawdle or hang around forever, either. Which is to say it would be pigheaded, plain foolish, not to take advantage of the moment to hear whatever he has to tell us.

He appears to wear a raggy bathrobe and old mules on his feet. I imagine he knows that, and realizes he might be taken for just one more of the hundreds of New York nut cases—the Broadway Viking and countless biblical shouters who tour the city spouting doomsday predictions. But one close look at our man, and it is clear that his robe is of the finest ancient silk, a dazzle of blues and greens, and his sandals are the desert itself.

I have much to ask him. Everyone does, for he already has drawn quite a crowd. We move in a scrum on Seventy-ninth, west from Amsterdam, peppering him with questions. Will the world go on? Do we have a future? What was Pharaoh really like? Did you see the face of God? He smiles and nods but does not break his stride. On God's face, he says it was pleasant but severe, the face of a circuit judge. A turned-up nose, he says. And Pharaoh? Just a dumb prick. Smooth talker. And the future of the world? I ask (it was I who asked that question in the first place). Will we survive? Ah, says Moses. You must be an artist. Only artists ask dumbass questions like that. Well, says the prophet, the world will continue on for many centuries. You might have asked *how* it will continue, in what state of being. That's a different matter.

At this point, a cop with a red face and tapping a billy club on his open palm approaches our group. What's all this? he asks. Various people pipe up. He's Moses, they say. Well, Mr. Moses, he says, you are disturbing the peace. That's what I do best, officer, says Moses. Be that as it may, says the cop, you have to move along.

So our entourage continues west along Seventy-ninth

Street, past Broadway and heading for West End Avenue. I was afraid the prophet might have forgotten my question. But after a while he speaks up again. Yes, he says, it is how the world will go on that you ought to be worried about. And judging from the way you have behaved so far, I'd say you were in the soup. Soup? says a lady in a mink stole. Soup? says a happy cobbler. Soup, says Moses. You already have fucked up mightily, he goes on. A regular shit storm. And I know from shit storms. God himself could not have imagined the damage you've done. So, God is a he? says a woman with a briefcase. I don't know, says Moses. I was with him only a minute or two. He might have been a she, I guess. The light was poor.

By now we've reached Riverside Drive, and the crowd has swelled to a thousand or more—everyone clamoring and elbowing everyone else to get closer to the old man. Is there something we can do to correct our course? I ask. No carbs, he says. Now, we all are at the river, where our leader walks to the end of a pier, makes swinging motions with his arms, and the waters of the Hudson part. Just like that. Anyone for New Jersey? he asks. At that, most of the crowd draws the line. But several jump in to follow the prophet, myself included.

THAT EVENING, a couple of sheets to the wind, I'll confess, I look up from my work and there was that picture of

Sarah. I was beginning to understand why Jack was having such a difficult time screwing his courage to tell the
girl he was dying. He was brave enough with his own ver-
dict, but he could not bear to break her heart. I studied the
picture a bit longer. The sentimental Irishman in me was
taking over for the old fart who ought to know better. A
crazy person is crazy all the time.

Bleary of eye, I hoist another sheet, and before you
know it, or I know it, I am calling up Jack and agreeing
to do what he had asked. The other end of the line is so
noisy with *Greats* and *Wonderfuls* and *Thank you thank you,
Mr. Murphy*s, had I not been staring at Sarah's picture, I
might have changed my mind again, bowed out even then.
Tomorrow? says Jack. I'll bring my car. Can we go out
tomorrow, Murph? I cannot tell you how grateful I am. Oh
sure you can, I say.

By the way, have you noticed that whenever someone
says "by the way," as if what he's about to tell you is an
incidental afterthought, it's really the thing he's wanted
to tell you all along? By the way, that explanation of my
willingness to be involved in the Jack and Sarah story
because I was intrigued and also because I had so little
else to do? That was only half true. The other half has
to do with the way I see the world, as equally beautiful
and ridiculous. I mean, take this Jack and Sarah business. A dying man can't muster the nerve to tell his wife
that he's dying, so he engages a stranger, a poet, to do it

for him. Absurd. No? But lovely too, and touching. And that, boyo, is life for you, is it not? A serious joke? Dr. Spector had me pegged. I am unable to participate in a sensible world wholeheartedly, which is why I dream things up. I said yes to Jack because I can't resist a serious joke.

How Well Are You Thinking?

Test devised by The Ohio State University

Please complete this form in ink without the assistance of others.

1. Name _____
2. Date of Birth ____/____/____
3. How far did you get in school? _____
4. I am a Man _____ Woman _____
5. I am Asian _____ Black _____ Hispanic _____ White _____ Other _____
6. Have you had any problems with memory or thinking? Yes ___ No ___ Only Occasionally ___
7. Have you had blood relatives with problems of memory or thinking? Yes ___ No ___
8. Do you have balance problems? Yes ___ No ___
9. Have you ever had a stroke? Yes ___ No ___
10. Do you currently feel sad or depressed? Yes ___ No ___ Only Occasionally ___

11. Have you had any changes in your personality?
    Yes ___ No ___

Dear The Ohio State University, I apologize for acting
counter to your instructions and completing your
form in purple crayon, rather than ink, but I thought
it might make my responses stand out from the pack,
offer a little flair. Know what I mean? As for the
assistance of others, I needed assistance only with
the first question. After that I flew like a donkey.
Best, Murph.

1. Thomas James Murphy. My parents named me
   Thomas, after Thomas More, James after James
   More, and Murphy after themselves.
2. 09/13/43. On the isle of Inishmaan, in the Aran
   Islands, in the west of Ireland. As soon as I saw
   where I was, I taught myself to stand and walk
   in an effort to escape, but was informed that
   they don't issue passports to babies. I explained
   that I'd be happy just to swim out and drown,
   but they told me everyone on Inishmaan says
   that.
3. As far as possible. Either in fact or in my mind.
   A teacher caught me daydreaming in class and
   asked me, Thomas, would you care to rejoin the
   group. I said, Not really.

4. Both. When my wife, Oona, was alive, I boasted that we had the America's first same-sex marriage. My friend Greenberg used to ask, which sex is that?

5. All the above, just like you, you racist bastards.

6. No, but I have had problems with drinking. The goddamn arthritis in my right hand makes it difficult to open the Jameson, so I smash the neck of the bottle on the kitchen counter, and hope no glass gets into the whiskey. You know how it is. Sometimes you just lose it. Like the time Woody Hayes, the coach of your football team at The Ohio State University, ran out on the field to tackle a player on the other team. You remember.

7. Yes. The blood relative who comes to mind is my uncle Brendan, who was kicked in the head trying to lift the rear end of a plough horse, to impress a girl named Maggie. The first use of the term *horse's ass* I believe. Brendan had a lot of problems with thinking.

8. Yes. I have balance problems with my checkbook. I can balance it on my nose while singing "The Mountains of Mourne" and smoking a stogie. But you probably don't mean that. My problems with balancing my checkbook usually stem from never knowing what I have in my account, which in turn leads to bouncing checks. I bounce better than

I balance. When Máire was little and we were dead broke (God knows why, there being so much money in poetry), I got a letter from one David d'Allesandro of the Chase National Bank, telling me that if I continued to write overdrafts, the bank would "find it inconvenient" to maintain my account. I wrote back, Dear Mr. d'Allesandro: If *you* find it inconvenient that I haven't any money, imagine how it is for my wife and daughter.

9. I had a stroke of genius once or twice, but it evaporated before I could get to the typewriter. Do you have strokes of genius at The Ohio State University? The addition of the article *The* before your name seems like such a stroke. I wonder if other institutions will follow suit, such as The Vanderbilt, and The Amherst.

10. Both. But don't worry about it, me Buckeyes.

11. No, but plenty of people wish I would. Are you among them?

ALL RIGHT. One time they don't know about. I forgot my area code. I was FedExing poems to the *Kenyon Review,* and you know? Where the FedEx form asks you for your phone number? I wrote down 122. That didn't look right, so I put 221, then 121. I stared at the numbers a minute, and finally asked the FedEx man, what's the area code for New York City? He gave no contempt with his answer. Oh, yes, I said. Sure. Thanks. I should have remembered it was a palindrome beginning with 2. Yeah, he said. A palindrome.

All right. Two. But that second time was different. I'm not sure if I forgot something, or if I was remembering something that didn't happen yet, like a dream. I was walking back to the Belnord, on Eighty-sixth between Central Park West and Columbus. Then I stopped, stood still. That much is fact. I don't know why I stopped, but I think I was scared or disoriented, the way one is when seated in a parked car in a parking lot, and the two cars on either side of you start to move backward. You think you are moving forward, but you are stock-still.

Well, that's what happened with me and Eighty-sixth Street. The entire boulevard liquefied and began to move toward me, like a whitewater river. As it flowed, it gained steam. I looked for something to grab on to, to keep from being swept away, but nothing presented itself—only me and the boulevard river rushing in the direction of the park, and making a godawful whooshing and gurgling noise, as it carried away TV repairmen, doctors, nannies, manicurists, policewomen, people who worked in Starbucks, dogs on leashes, and all the denizens of Eighty-sixth Street, everyone shouting and barking and waving arms in a desperate effort to remain afloat. There followed fire hydrants, trucks, buses, and larger debris

still—huge trees and an entire town house, all rushing
down the rapids. Withal, I managed to stand my ground,
expecting the river to gobble me up too, but it did not.
And then it was gone, just like that, and Eighty-sixth
Street was back to its original shape. Pedestrians were
staring at me as they passed, wondering if I were ill. A
beer delivery guy was the only one to stop and ask, Mis-
ter? You okay? I said, Maybe.

SEE HERE, BUCKEYES. How sure are you about memory,
anyway? Is it always applied to what you remember? For
instance, I've always suspected that Shakespeare was
really Charles Darwin. Or vice versa. I never know how
one should put it. Oh, I appreciate that Bacon and Mar-
lowe are assumed to be the chief contenders, since it's
unthinkable that Shakespeare could have been Shakespeare. But, no offense, how obvious can you get. Anyone
could name a literary contemporary of Shakespeare's
and call him Shakespeare. Nothing to it. It takes someone with a real nose for crime to figure out that while
Darwin was writing *The Origin of Species* in the nineteenth century, he was also polishing off *Hamlet* in the
seventeenth. At first I merely surmised that only a man
like Darwin had the sort of genius Shakespeare had,
that is, the galactic imagination to perceive and declare
connections among invisible stages of development. But

then I found an actual clue, a typo in *Hamlet*. "To be or not to be" was intended to read "To be *and* not to be." There you go.

Do you follow? What if memory does not apply to the past, after all, but rather to something that will occur tomorrow or next week, and the past is something we only forget? And that would be grand, 'cause most of what we can remember is terrible. Looking back on our lives, we don't stand a ghost of a chance. But looking ahead to our past, why, ma'am, you've won the lottery. For all you know, the things you remember haven't happened yet. Small wonder you're confused. This is bound to affect your actions and decisions, because if you base either or both on your recollection of something occurring tomorrow or next week, you're bound to screw up. Yet even that conclusion would be based on projected memory. One thing, though. If memory is unusable in the traditional way, the mania for daily slaughter might be reduced. We Irish would lose our grudges. Unthinkable. History could not be held responsible for repeating itself. As a bonus, we would not need to hear that droning quote from Santayana anymore.

Which brings me to that old bird I'm passing at Eighty-sixth and Broadway right now. What if I only think of him as old because that's how he appears to me. My memory tells me that he is how an old man looks. He looks like me. But if my memory of such categories has not happened yet, then neither has he, and he cannot be old. Why, he's a kid. A spring chicken. I don't look old to him, either. I, too, am a spring chicken. We cluck good morning to each other. There are two ways to look at people, I think. One way is as they are. One is as they will be. That old bird at Eighty-sixth and Broadway. He'll be learning to sit up and crawl soon. Not long after that, he'll stand and walk. Good for him.

Which brings me to that girl Sarah, whom I have not met. Yet I have met her picture, snapped in the past. We are old friends who have yet to make each other's acquaintance. Sarah, do you recall what I started to say to you?

We have to rethink this whole business of time. Don't you agree, Buckeyes? I mean, since time does not exist and never has, we ought to reconsider the entire question. Remember two months from now? Maybe it's language that confines us. We simply do not have the language to deal with the past in the future. We don't have the grammatical tense. If we did, we might say some remarkable things in our beautiful garbled new tongue. The language spoken in the world's not. And everyone would listen to our language, because it speaks the truth, and people would learn from it when they grow young again, and eventually are born. We must love the world. Is that not so, my Buckeyed friends? I refuse to budge from my trance.

IN THEIR TRANCE, the grown-ups sat in concentric circles in a field, the men in the inner circle, the women in the outer. Have I told you about this? We children were excluded, but were permitted to watch. What good these ancient harvest rituals were supposed to accomplish confused me, since the only crop I ever saw on Inishmaan was potatoes, and little enough of that, studding the land like the rocks. Still, the grown-ups prayed, like their Druid ancestors, year after year. They were more successful when they asked divine powers for fish, the invisible crop that seduced men to the ocean, where many died. Synge caught the repetitive sadness of the island fisherman in *Riders to the Sea*—the relentless scraping of the curraghs on the pebbles, looking like the shells of mussels, but heavy. Four big men at a time hauling the boats to a place on the shore where the vessels could float. The men would climb aboard and wobble out, slowly out and slowly back, if ever they came back.

In their circle in the field, the men sat bobbing back and forth as if at sea themselves, like the davening of Jews of which I learned from Greenberg much later in America—bodies rocking, keening for the dead, and for their lives. The women surrounding them did the same. They wore hats of red and brown wool, and their great arms glistened in the moonlight that beamed behind the ribs of the clouds. They prayed in Irish, the lilt of the rhythms lifting up and down in the human circles, rising and falling like boats. At the top of a hill, a thick gray horse halfheartedly grazed.

Outside the two circles we children played like sprites and ghostly figures. We dressed up as animals, I don't remember why. It wasn't part of the ritual, I'm pretty sure of that. Perhaps one child did it once, long ago, and the custom caught on. We dressed as goats and hares and sheep and unreal animals too, satyrs and unicorns, in a concocted mythology. The liquid shapes of us moving about the shadows, and the moaning of our parents and grandparents. One year I was a boar. Another, a wolf. One time a ram. I snorted and spat like a ram. I spoke the language of rams.

What all this looked like from above, I cannot imagine. The elders prayed under the sighs of the moon. I remember thinking, What sort of God would be moved by such a sight? What God would be impressed by the prayers of a people as small and miserable as my own? In the center of the circle of the men a turf fire burned in dull ashes. It neither flared nor tapered nor extinguished itself, but held to a steady warmth and its shifting colors of red and brown. After several hours, the gray smoke generated by the fire rose and settled on the people like a cloud descended. It filled our noses, ears, our eyeballs. My senses were filled with smoke.

The night I was a ram I met a bull. Timmy Leary was the bull. His horns were alder branches. While the grown-ups prayed, we had it out head to head on the dead plain, near an outcropping of chipped rocks. We stalked each other as the moon swirled around us. On a patch of frozen rainfall I got him down, though Timmy was bigger, a wide table of a kid. Still, I gathered up my ramness, lowered my great round horns, and hit him hard in the stomach. He hit his head on a rock, and was dazed. Lying on his back he eventually opened his eye like an owl's, and I picked up a rock, as if I were about to kill him. Timmy Leary, the sweet laughing boy, who never did me a moment's harm. As we were walking back to the circles of grown-ups, he asked me why I did that. I told him, It wouldn't be you I was killing, it would be them. *Them?* he said. But by then I had left him to go his own way, and I turned toward the cliff over the skull of the sea.

DEAR MR. MORPHY,

We at AARP have checked our records and note that you have never chosen to join our ranks. Mr. Morphy, we are taking this opportunity, once again, to ask you to be a valued part of AARP. We see that you are seventy-two years young. If you are in good mental and physical health—and we certainly hope you are—our actuarial charts indicate that you will live another twenty years, perhaps more. So, Mr. Morphy, don't you think it's time that you joined the tens of millions of Americans in AARP, enjoying the many benefits of membership? All you need do is check YES on the enclosed card. After that, AARP will do its best to make your next twenty years the happiest of your life. Best wishes from your friends at AARP.

Dear AA,

Forgive the informal address. The reason I never have joined AARP is that you don't have a clubhouse. I only join clubs with clubhouses. And you're not exclusive enough. I like clubs that exclude left and right, and hurt people's feelings. As for my next twenty years, I seriously doubt that they will be the happiest of my life, unless, of course you can bring back my wife, Oona, and my friend Greenberg. If resurrection is included among your many benefits, sign me up. Otherwise, I simply have too much on my plate at the moment. That is, when I don't spill half of it on the floor. Much as I would love to join my fellow members in Malaysian cooking classes and games of Mad Libs, what with my sudden urge to skin mules, split rails, and raise dead beets, well, where's the time? To be sure, my mental health seems to be in question at the moment, so you never know. I may change what's left of my mind. One more thing? It's Murphy, not Morphy, though I admire your suggestion of change by the spelling. And I must tell you, seeing Morphy in print is so attractive, Morphy it will be from this day forward. Thank you, AA.

Best wishes from your friends near the bone yard,

Morph.

MURPH? I've been thinking about our plan. Jack picks me up at my apartment house in his red Corvair, and is making the turn off Second, heading for the Queensboro Bridge. I start to tell him that I've been thinking about it too, and am getting cold feet, when he says he thinks that one visit with Sarah would be too abrupt. I mean, I bring a stranger home for dinner, a guy I met in a bar, and he's here to tell my wife that she'll be without a husband in a couple of months. I know what I said about you having the words, Murph. But maybe I didn't think it through. I ask him what he's getting at. Well, he says, what would you think of this being just a first visit, where you and Sarah get to know each other a little. And then, after four or five more visits, when you've become more of a friend of the family, so to speak, you and I can sit down with her and lower the boom. Lower the boom, indeed, I tell him. I wish you'd thought of this before, Jack. I'd have held to my no, and sent you packing. Now you're asking me to become part of your household, you and Sarah.

He goes quiet and looks ashamed, like a little boy who had misplaced an expensive gift. I remind myself that the poor slob is dying. Now we are across the bridge and into Woodside. I know there's no turning back, and I'm still curious to meet Sarah of the bittersweet smile. I want to look at her. So, I tell Jack not to worry. I will meet Sarah today, enjoy my dinner, I'm sure . . . Oh, yeah, she's a kick-ass cook, says Jack . . . and then we'll all sit down together the second time I visit, and, as you say, lower the boom, as gently as possible. But we must tell her that this was our arrangement from the start, Jack. That this is what you wanted me to do, and that's why I was doing it. If we're up front with her, she's likely to appreciate the trouble you took, and how careful you have been about her feelings. And, Jack? I give him my coldest Irish stare. There will be only one more time, not four or five. He nods. I understand, he says. I nod too, more unsure than ever of what I'm getting myself into.

There's something else you should know about Sarah, says Jack. I think, She's deaf? She reads like crazy, he says. She went to a fancy college. Smith. In Massachusetts. Ever hear of it? Oh, sure you have. Can you beat that? he says. She's blind and she sails through Smith College at the top of her class. God knows what she saw in me. Need, I suggest. That's what she said, Murph! Need! I never knew if she meant hers or mine. You two really are going to hit it off! Anyway, she's an amazing reader. Has a thousand books in braille. And, I don't know, a million books on tape. When I told her you were coming for dinner, she mentioned a title of one of your books, or poems, I don't know which. Just like that. Off the top of her head. She knows everything you've written. He goes on talking talking talking.

You can see I'm nervous, he says. I tell him I'm nervous too. He chuckles. Maybe Sarah is the only one of the three of us who isn't nervous, Murph. She's a calm sort of person. Inside. Serene, I offer. Yeah. That's the word. *Serene.* See? I knew you were the man for this job. A few minutes more and we pull into a driveway beside a squat two-story wood-and-brick house, which looks like a sad passing thought. Here we are, says Jack, a pig in shit.

YOU'RE ASKING YOURSELF how we got together, aren't you, Murph? He passes the roast. Sure you are. Everyone does. Everyone wonders how a dashing, sophisticated fellow such as myself got hooked up with a lumbering brute like Sarah. It was like this. In the summer of 2005, I was working as a lifeguard at the big beach in East Hampton. I was young, tan, ripped, you get the picture. It was early one Saturday morning, long before the crowds came out, and I was getting the lifeguard stand ready, stacking the

PFDs, and lugging out the big yellow umbrellas for the rich, arranging the towels, stuff like that. It couldn't have been six-thirty yet, when out of the corner of my eye I see this long-legged beauty walking toward the ocean. Stepping slow and careful, as if she's in her sleep, not running the way most of the younger people do. So I went on with my work, but I kept an eye on her at the same time. She was wearing a dark blue one-piece suit, and with that dusty gold hair of hers and those legs, I can tell you, it wasn't hard to keep watching. Then, as she's standing ankle-deep in the water, out of nowhere, a wave, maybe ten feet high, comes up and knocks her out of my sight. So I ran like crazy. The wave receded, and she was lying faceup on the pebbles, out cold. Like the superhero I am, I picked her up on my arms and carried her to dry sand, and gave her mouth-to-mouth. I'm not sure it was necessary, you know, but I wanted to get my mouth on hers, if you get my drift. And whack! She hauls off and slaps me. I'm telling you, Murph. She's small, but she packs a punch. She knocked me on my backside. Me! And then, if you believe it, she stands, extends her little hand and pulls me up.

Hey! I tell her. I was saving your life. Is that what you call it? she says. I laughed, and she laughed, and only then could I see she was blind. Later, she'd tell our friends, why else would I have fallen for Jack. Had to be *blind*. Isn't that right, babe? I tell her that she ought not to be coming to the beach alone, the way she is. And what does she say, Murph? She says, Everyone's alone, which told me then and there I was way out of my class. She says she lives with her folks just down the road from the beach, and she's been coming there ever since she was a kid, and no hulking ape of a lifeguard was going to tell her different, and why don't I mind my own business. Not a word about almost drowning, you understand. And I call her a stuck-up ungrateful bitch, and she smiles that amazing smile, and I ask her out, and she says, Anywhere but the movies. And that was that. I won't tell you how hard a time her folks gave us, or how I first had her in her own bedroom while her folks were fighting downstairs. Maybe later. But that's our story, Murph. And when anyone asks how we got together, I tell them, She swept me off my ass.

Throughout the length of Jack's dinner table mono-logue, Sarah smiles her dark chocolate smile from time to time, but says not a word. While listening to Jack, I mainly hear her silence.

NOISELESS, I have drawn my straw pallet to lie on the floor beside my da's bed. Above me, he breathes like the polar sea. He floats in his sleep. I would like to ride the current with him—the two of us on a mare heading to deep waters, under the sea's sun. But he is alone in his dying, as I am alone in my living. I lie on my makeshift bed, my arms behind my head like angel wings. Every so often, I

look up. He begins to appear as glass, as a glass ink bottle
into which I may dip my pen. I dip my pen in my father and
write what he tells me. "Ah penny, brown penny, brown
penny." And now I am reborn, a new child again, learning
to make my way in the new world. What is a rock? What is
a daisy? Hours pass and I crawl around the poem I write of
him and me. Soon I pull myself upright, vertical man, and
I write of that, as my father instructs me. Automatic writing. Then it stops, and there are no further instructions,
so I put down my pen and cap the ink bottle, resting my
head on the parchment of his arms.

MY HEAD HURTS, Oona. Too much TV, even in the daytime. Daytime TV. And not just TCM, either. Everything.
Quiz shows. Would you believe it? I'm a gamer. I'm a goner.
Yesterday morning, I watched *Let's Make a Deal,* followed
by a movie with Ronald Colman. I don't mean I watched
it in the company of Ronald Colman. He's dead, as you
know. (Do you miss my uproarious wit?) The movie—it
had *harvest* in the title—was about a World War I dough-
boy (Colman), who lost his memory in a battle, and was
put in a mental hospital, from which he escapes. He wanders into the nearby town and meets Greer Garson, who
loves him on the spot, memory or no memory. They marry
and live in a typical woolly little English cottage, where he
becomes a writer. Have you noticed, Oona, how fucking

easy it is to become a writer, according to fiction? You just sit down and scribble with some music playing behind you, and presto, you're Wallace Stevens. So, naturally, Colman is great at it off the bat, and he sells his first piece to a magazine in Liverpool. The editor summons him to Liverpool to praise his work and give him more assignments. As if an editor would ever do something nice like that. Anyway, as he is crossing a street in Liverpool, he's hit by a car, and at once his memory is restored. Turns out that he's landed gentry. Now having no memory of Greer Garson or the woolly cottage, he returns to his ancestral home, where he is much loved and a real big shot. His picture appears in the papers, and is seen by Greer, who goes to him but does not tell him she's his wife, or anything of their former life together. Instead she takes the position of his secretary, and serves nobly. Well, wouldn't you know it? One day Colman finds himself in Liverpool again, and he is disturbed by vague recollections. I can't remember exactly how he and Greer wind up at their old wooly cottage, but they do, and when everything floods back to Colman, and Greer is assured that he remembers her at last, and loves her, they embrace. The End. Jesus, Oona. Can you lose your memory just like that? Tell you one thing, darlin'. I'd never forget I loved you. You wouldn't let me. You'd hit me with a car first. Anyway, that was that. Máire called to check on me, as she always does. A Jameson and a good weep, and so to bed.

AT TWO in the morning, I appear on *Let's Make a Deal*. The host is Wallace Stevens. And here he is, says the offstage announcer. The Manecdote of the Anecdote, the Caviar of the Clavier, the Emperor of Ex Tempore . . . The curtain parts and there's old Stevens in his tweeds and stripes. He scans the studio audience like a sniper. I try to hide under the humongous sombrero they gave me before the show. Maybe he'll just see the hat and ignore me. No such luck. Who's there, under that handsome sombrero? he asks no one in particular. Is that you, Señor Murphy? The audience shrieks and applauds. Stevens drags me to the stage.

Standing beside him, I look like an orange mushroom. Thomas Murphy! says Stevens, presenting me to the crowd. There is much cheering. Thomas Murphy, ladies and gentlemen! So, what's it to be, Murph? He points to stage left, where a redhead in a silver dress is posing first before a barrel, then a curtain, and finally a huge black box, a seven- or eight-foot cube. Stevens drapes his tweedy arm over my shoulder. The barrel, the curtain, or the box?

Box! Box! Box! yells the audience. I'll take the box, I say, meekly. More wild cheering. Murph, says Stevens, what would you say if I told you that there is one million dollars in that barrel. Will you still take the box? Box! Box! Box! Louder than ever. I repeat, Box. Murph, says Stevens, what would you say if I told you that behind that curtain is a new hot tub (cheers), a new barbecue (cheers), a new car (more cheers), and it's all for you to enjoy in your *new home*, the Isle of Capri? And I don't mean *on* the Isle of Capri, Murph. I mean, the whole isle. It's yours! If the price is right. Oh no, that's a different show. The audience howls. So, what do you say, Thomas Murphy? The curtain or the box? Before the crowd can yell Box Box Box again, I say Box, and everyone starts clapping rhythmically.

Well, says Stevens, you've said no to the barrel and a million dollars. And no to the curtain and the Isle of Capri. So, let's see what's in the box. He opens the front wall like a door, and there is nothing in the huge black container. Now the crowd is hysterical with pleasure, and Stevens smiles and thwacks me on the shoulder. You've done it, Murph, he says. You've chosen the prize of prizes, the best deal we've ever offered. But the box is empty, I say, sounding like a disappointed little boy. Empty? says Stevens. Empty? Why, Thomas Murphy, where are your eyes, man? The box is full! Full of you! And with that he shoves me inside, and closes the box. The audience has gone silent. Inside the box, it is black as pitch, and I'm suffused with the odor of turf. Then I hear a noise. Stevens is slipping me a note through the mail slot in the wall. It reads, And your poetry is shit, too.

TU FU (A.D. 712–770), Chinese poet, wrote of his lack of recognition in his own lifetime. Other poets praised his talent, but he lived in a humble house, hungry, his clothing one notch above tatters. Servants, he said, treated him with disdain. His fellow poets, too, lived this way. They knew one another's work, but their fame went no further than their small circle. I read a translation of "To Pi Ssu Yao," the poem on which this information about Tu Fu's life is given, and I cannot tell if the poet means to lament or boast. Closer to a boast, I think, an expression of satisfaction that the quality of his work and that of his contemporaries will be sufficient recompense for him. That his poems will be handed down to "descendants" consoles him. What then did I, neither hungry, poor, nor ill-clothed, who lives in eleven rooms, and is well known enough to win a reading here and a prize there—what did I make of that?

In the back of the taxi I go over my acceptance speech, delighting in its wit and flow, its mixing of sincerity and self-effacement, the warming anecdote, the dip into a pun, the soar into high seriousness here and there, a splash of poetry, a flash of skin. Then I crumple the pages, and leave them on the taxi floor. Here's what I want: When they announce my name, I want to approach the podium in concentration camp stripes, and tell them nothing. Not even my serial number. But in reality, of course, when the time comes, I rise from my ballroom chair, curtsy left and right, and smile like a baby. The master of ceremonies pats me on the head, powders my bottom, changes me, and sends me back to my chair. About prizes? Blake never won one.

WHEREAS TODAY I WALK the city with my head dug in like a plough, mired. I hate these moods, their selfishness, grotesque. Around me march my beautiful New Yorkers with their cowled faces, flayed by the wind, fresh from their vile mills. They hear the drumming of real graves, while I, fancy me, indulge myself in a pastime. Greenberg would have ribbed me without mercy. Oona too. Me too. Snap out of it, Murph. In a day, an hour, I will be on a high again, thrilled to the bone to be permitted life and poetry, thrilled to have Máire with me and to be able to read William to sleep twice a week—while they, my beautiful New Yorkers, have not the luxury of mood swings. Or of moods at all, for Chrissake. Courage with resignation. That's their bloody mood. One mood forever. How I adore them, though I would not tell them so, lest I sound patronizing, as if I were accepting them, when the opposite is true. They accept me. Me, the freakish exception to the rules of their existence. What one must do as a poet, before placing the right words in the right order, before wandering lonely as a cloud or summoning a second coming, is to recognize the precious gift of one's perch, and then walk with one's fellow citizens and feel their powerless power. I push my body into my beautiful New Yorkers, and vanish with them in the brown, humiliating earth.

TO WIT. On my way to an interview at a newspaper the following morning, I stopped to talk with a woman on a stoop on Seventy-seventh Street. I took her for my ma. She asked where I was going, and when I told her, she said I must be an important person. No, I said. Just a poet. Oh, she said. Me, too. But I have yet to write my poems down, she said. They're all in my head. A fine place to be, I offered, and she smiled a toothless smile. She told me she'd been a singer in a nightclub, a chantoosie at the Copa. Do you know "What Are You Doing the Rest of Your Life?" I asked her. She started to sing it in a cigarette voice. Naturally, I joined in. We chatted on. She had a daughter somewhere, who had been taken from her in the hospital in Baltimore where she'd given birth as a teenager. Many years ago, she had traced the girl to Albany, but never caught up with her. The woman was married once, to a no-good cornet player, she said. Lasted less than a year. How do you manage to live? I said. I work nights at a tollbooth on the Staten Island side of the Verrazano Bridge, she said. Do people ever talk to you, or do they just pay the toll and go? Sometimes they talk, she said. About the weather, or the traffic. Once in a while they ask directions. I gave her some money and sat with her a while longer, and could no longer recall where I had originally been headed. To an interview at a newspaper, she reminded me.

MY MA, black cookie jar, hauls potatoes on her back, holding the twisted end of the sack in her fist and letting the weight of the potatoes fall below her shoulders. Sitting flat on her head is the kind of straw hat they put on horses for a joke, with the ears sticking out of holes in the brim. Ma does not smile. Her big eyes greet her tasks. The black jacket, the black skirt, down to the black-laced shoes. I never see her in fancy dress. The closest she comes is Sunday mass, when she and the other women sit in church on one side, while my da and the men sit on the other. The women are broader than the men, broader shoulders. Like rakes and pitchforks, they are built for the work they do. On that day only, Ma wears the red plaid shawl her mother wore. Otherwise, black. I have a grainy photo taken in the 1930s before I was born, by a Kodak Klito box camera, a plate-changing model. Ma is standing with a neighbor's child, holding her hand, the girl looking at the camera, Ma studying the ground. Once in a while, I'd catch her looking at my da, with nothing in her look. No love. No question. Your ma's as strong as a horse, Mickey Dailey said to me in the schoolyard. I popped him in the nose.

REGRETS? ASKS THE KID from the newspaper. In your long distinguished career, Mr. Murphy, do you have any regrets? To which I reply, beguiling as ever, Sonny, I'm going to travel inside you for a while, and let you feel the gravel I shovel in your blood, and the bulge and beat I cause in your pulse, as I run amok among your tissues, go at your muscles with a paring knife, your every inner town and village unbulwarked against my assaults. I shall practice debauchery in the caves of your lymph nodes, terrorism in your viscera, barbarism in your glands. I shall scrape out your spleen, plough snow around your kidneys, and invite the monkey on your back to brachiate from vein to vein, all in an effort to cause as much pain as you can endure, more in fact. I shall assail your entrails, cause tumors on your humors, sup on your heart, and fling my empty oyster shells smack against your brain, which I then will toss out into the street for lack of payment of rent. When I have done all that to give you a taste of how the real world suffers, then see if you have the nerve to ask me: Regrets?

UNTITLED
    for Oona
    (draft)

        Or is it the wood I am thinking of,
        And only transform it into the bright bird

Because I dread the wood?
The mind does that—tipped and bent
From its fears, it whistles past the graveyard
Toward the field. My dynasties are vague,
Old Irishmen and their tillable lives,
Tilting over ploughs. Rust. Broken blades
In the furrows. Them.

I know little of their language, nothing
Of their haunts. But something of their terrors—
The genome has bequeathed me that.
In your cupped hand I rest
For a spell, until I lapse from
The theology of love, remember the wood,
And reach for the bright bird.

WOULD THAT I could dream up a new style of writing that would effect a new style of living. I mean, we so-called creative writers do not actually create anything. We simply respond to that which already has been created. But if we *could* create something, I'd like to do it through style. A new style, never tried before, the style of the world's not that merely by its own existence, by the statement of itself, made religions obsolete, and nations as well, and everything else that has gummed up the works since the works began. Everything we think of now as normally stupid and lethal, would be made old hat in a sweep by a different arrangement of words. The orderly powers of government giving way to accidental lilies. A different rhythm. Like jazz. Like Sonny Rollins at the Williamsburg Bridge. The words themselves wouldn't cut it, not beautiful words any more than beautiful music or beautiful art, which have the staying power of butterflies. Goebbels in tears at Wagner. Wagner in tears at himself. But a style of writing so revolutionary that it insists upon horses mixing with their own shadows and the shingles of the sea, gray and blue, sudsing up at the base of the Freedom Tower, with no comment, no announcement, with nothing justified or explained, well, that would be something. Too much to ask? I think not, my liege. We stumble upon improvement, from time to time.

I recall the night Jesus was born. I was tending sheep in the Belnord, and the wolves were pacing back and forth and licking their chops. Were it not for a new style of behavior in the air, they would have trussed up the pint-size Savior and gulped him down for lunch—blood, body, and all. Instead they murmured something about a new style of behavior and trotted on. You were there. You know it's true. We have started out badly, but who knows.

Poetry is the product of an effort to invent a world appreciably better than the one we live in. Its

> essence is not the representation of the facts, but the deliberate concealment and denial of the facts.
> —H. L. Mencken, in Thomas Murphy's
> *Book of Dandy Quotations*

SOMETIMES I FORGET what a delightfully curious fellow I am. And then I do something that reminds me. This morning, for instance, I took down every one of my poetry books—others' books, not my own—from the floor-to-ceiling bookcase reserved for poetry, in the front hall. I took them down one at a time and I opened each to a random page. There must be seven or eight hundred books on my shelf—from old Tu Fu to Yiddish poems to the work of Phillis Wheatley, Edgar Guest, Julie Sheehan, William Empson, Daniel Halpern, Marianne Moore, and others. I have 'em all. I laid all the open books on the floor of the hallway, with a foot or two between the rows, so that I could patrol the lot of them and read a line or two on each open page. Sometimes I happened to open a book to a complete poem, sometimes to isolated stanzas. I read the lines aloud, as if the entire haphazard arrangement on the floor constituted one very long organized poem.

So, I read some lines of Shakespeare, then moved on to Carl Philips, thence to Poe, thence to Countee Cullen, and Billy Collins, and Emily Dickinson and Frost and Southey, and Galway Kinnell, and on and on. There were no connections among the passages, and nothing made continuous sense. But the accumulation of the total work had an effect, nonetheless—like a collection of all the comments one might hear from a crowd viewing a monument, Lenin's Tomb, for instance, or coming upon an amazing natural sight, say, Niagara Falls. All the various things visitors ever said to one another when expressing appreciation of Niagara Falls, rising in and filling my front hall from floor to ceiling.

I shouted "the wound is open" from Anne Sexton. I shouted "the mad in absolute power" from X. J. Kennedy. I shouted "it was not a heart, beating" from Sylvia Plath, and "I remember these things I still remember them" from Apollinaire, and "some things are truly lost" from Richard Wilbur, and "went you to conquer?" from Donne. I shouted "what is articulated strengthens itself" from Miłosz. I loved that so much, I shouted it twice. The exercise occupied most of the morning, if you include the time I used in taking down the books and putting them back. Afterward, I sat in the kitchen, with my toast and coffee, pleased with myself, I don't know why. I can't recall thinking about the poets' lines I'd read. I was not studying them, and they certainly were not studying me. Principally, I was more aware of the sound the accumulated lines made, senseless, illogical, beautiful. What is articulated strengthens itself. We simply had been keeping company with one another,

comforting one another, me and my fellow poets, in the
morning, in the front hall.

"WHAT OLD MEN dream / Is pure restatement of the original theme, / A sense of rootedness, a source held near
and dear." My C. Day-Lewis shout.

WHEN THE SICKNESS was devouring Oona as she lay
like a queen in our palatial bedroom—devouring her at
such a rate that you could see the body wither as you sat
with her—I asked did she recall the time of her past good
health. She said she could no more recall being robust
than she could, in health, recall the pain and lassitude of
illness. If we were able to return to the past in body as well
as in mind, she said, that would be grand. But it is part
of nature's unfairness that we can remember that we were
healthy at an earlier time, without feeling any of it. It is
like a story someone read to us a long long time ago. All
the days before this blight, she said, are a throng of lights
on a shore at night. And I am a boat borne out.

IF GREEN-WOOD was good enough for Henry Ward
Beecher, Louis Tiffany, Leonard Bernstein, Boss Tweed,
and the Wizard of Oz (Frank Morgan to you), it was good

enough for Oona. So we buried her there among the swells, where she lay, the swellest of the lot. In the nineteenth century, they said it was the ambition of every New Yorker to live on Fifth Avenue, take "airings" in Central Park, and sleep in Green-Wood, in Brooklyn. At least we'd satisfied the airings part, and when we stood around her fresh grave—Máire, William, Greenberg, and me—Greenberg noted that the place was so beautiful, with its fabric hills and old trees and justly self-satisfied Victorian monuments, it looked as if Oona was in heaven already.

This afternoon, William has brought a red helium-filled balloon to send to his grandmother in that older heaven. Just three of us now, we stand about the grave site, William holding his balloon until the moment he deems right. Máire takes my hand, and says nothing. I say nothing myself. I can hear Oona chuckling—so it took this to keep you quiet. The great trees, stark in winter, stand stolid, as if bracing themselves for an inevitable wind. The silence of the others buried here feels respectful. More of the dead lie in this place than the residents of Green-Wood. Before this land became a formal cemetery, it was the site of the Battle of Long Island, eventually lost by Washington and his men, some of whom lie here too, but in the long run, a victory. The stupid Brits took so long winning here, they exhausted their forces. Americans lost the battle, yet you know the rest.

We mark the first anniversary of Oona's death. It was

William's idea. He asked if we could go. He and Oona didn't get on in the way that William and I get on, man to clone. She was clearly a superior grown-up, the one to turn to if a T-shirt was on backward or a shoe had been lost in the trash, or when a Band-Aid required someone to put it on right. He called her Toona, deliberately. You think I'm a fish? she said to him. Well, you look a little like a fish, Grandma, William said. But I heard someone called a Big Tuna on TV. He was the boss. So I'm going to call you Toona, 'cause you're the boss. Give us a kiss, she said.

Máire has brought roses, which she places on the dark earth of the grave. I think, a red rag on a hedge. Something I saw in Inishmaan a long time ago. A red rag on a hedge. William says, I'm going to send this to Toona now. And he releases the red balloon into the sky. About a hundred feet up it is caught by a breeze, and it dances in the air like a lantern swung by the train conductor at the end of a caboose. The breeze then carries the balloon to the naked branches of a tall tree, where it snags. Oh, William cries in disappointment. Give it a minute, Máire tells him. Sure enough, the balloon is soon blown free, and shoots up straight to Toona.

NOTHIN' TO IT, our original threesome. There was nothing to it. Miles. Queen. The Huckabee dance, in which I

stomped around the kitchen stooped like Groucho, singing, Huckabee for President, instead of Wintergreen. A
day trip to Carthage. Another to Troy. Elvis on the phone
for you, Máire. Who bought this orange-scented soap?
Who bought these vegetables? Let's declare world peas.
Dad, I'm going to marry Dennis Rodman. Me too, says
Oona. Me too, says I. Trivial Pursuit. Significant Pursuit.
I hate my teacher. Okay, my girl. I'll kill her. Dad, can I
watch? Take Your Daughter to Work Day. Where should I
take her, Oona? To your desk. Yakety yak, night and day.
Standing outside the front door one night, Greenberg
wondered if we were throwing a party. What did the man
say as he walked past the sad horse? Hey, Mom, Dad's
drunk again. Get the bottle, dear. Let's join him. He said,
Why the long face? This is the worst kale I ever et. Is there
any other kind? Draw us a cello. Draw us some Jell-O. A
Jell-O cello. This is not a pipe? Sure, it's a pipe. Are you
blind? That's a *pipe*. Dad, what's a courtesan? A Porta
Potti for judges. Are the two of you ever coming to dinner? NO! Dad, the toilet's cracked. Psycho-ceramic? And
a missing-forever flashlight and an uncooked turkey at
Thanksgiving and a jig in the Vatican and no waste. There
was no waste, you see. Downtown subway run all night?
Doo da, doo da. You should have seen us on a good day. I
don't remember any others. Our trip on the QE2. Dad! I'm
so excited to see Ireland. Darlin', everyone is, until they
get there.

OUR LIFE BEGINS in dreams, but does not stay with them. Think of the days it took for the crossing from Ireland to America. I stood at the ship's brass railing and addressed the sea, rippling and throbbing like my heart's blood. What if my ship never reached its destination? What if the old European fools were right, and there was no other side to sail to? Only those bucktoothed dragons and a cliff wall, emptying down to a hell of ice and shoveled ashes. The ship chugs on blithely to the edge of nothing. Or else, what if there were no end to the voyage at all? On and on forever. No dragons, no cliffs, no shore to come to? Would I make use of the endless space? I wondered. Would I inscribe poems on it? Eventually, I assured myself that the ship's engines would slow to a murmur and I would see the harbor lights. What would I be doing the rest of my life?

In a championship fight with George Foreman, Muhammad Ali was beating Foreman badly, and was trash-talking him all the way. In a clinch near the end of the fight, Ali taunted the exhausted Foreman, "This would be a bad time to get tired," he said. Tired? Not yet. Not hitting the canvas just yet.

IF I SIT DOWN will I get up? That is the question. Others might say, What's a legally dead old jackass like me doing participating in a sit-in protesting the use of horse-drawn carriages in Central Park? As protests go, this one is pretty penny ante, certainly as compared with the civil rights protests of fifty years ago, or women's rights protests, or the ones for farmworkers. Something was at stake in those to-dos, other than a horse's well-being. And if you want to know the cruel truth, horses aren't the smartest animals in the world anyway, which I know for having grown up beside 'em and on top of 'em and sometimes under 'em, as they'd as soon throw you as take a jump. They probably don't mind pulling these carriages. They might need the work. So, I must tell you, it's not the particular issue that has me sitting cross-legged where the unplowed snow clings to the sidewalk. It's the principle. Civil rights is civil rights, two-legged or four. Still, as the news people like to put it, the question remains: If I sit down will I get up?

Out of the corner of my eye I spot Arthur. He trots laboriously along Central Park West, head down, a huge bale of fur. I call out to him. Arthur! Arthur the Bear! He proceeds without looking up.

The others sitting here are younger. (Who isn't?) When they're not shivering and burying their heads in their scarves and coat collars, they give me smiles and fist bumps. I try to dredge up the old passions that went with sitting in at Woolworth's in the 1960s. Come to think of it, that was where I met Greenberg, the mere recollection of which warms me to the present occasion. One of the protest organizers has brought a roan, bay and sorrel in color, a dour little thing no more than thirteen hands, tied to a lamppost and standing in the street, with its head stuck in a bucket of feed. A white fur diamond dominates its forehead. To its bridle a hand-drawn sign has been affixed: FREE ME. If the poor beast wants anything, I suppose it's to go back to what it was originally. (Who doesn't?) So I'm on its side. That's all civil rights means anyway—returning to a state of natural dignity. The movements are called revolutionary, but they're really restorative. All we ever wanted in Ireland was to be Irish.

Thinking about that Ali-Foreman fight, I remember reading a story in Richard Wright's *Black Boy*, about when he was a young man in Memphis, grinding lenses in an eyeglass factory. His supervisor told him that Harrison, a black coworker, held a grudge against Wright. It wasn't true. The white men in the factory were trying to instigate a boxing match between the two black boys, for their own sick entertainment. At first, Wright and Harrison refused. But the white men persisted, eventually offering them five dollars apiece to put on the fight. Thinking it easy money, the two finally agreed, and the match took place in a basement on a Saturday afternoon, before an all-white crowd shouting obscenities. The boys jabbed lightly at first, pulling punches, then they punched harder, then a lot harder, until they'd beaten each other senseless. After the fight, they were full of shame and would not speak to each other. In the end they'd become the enemies the white subhumans had said they were in the beginning, turning a lie into the truth. Wright and Harrison had allowed themselves to be degraded to the level of the white scum who had goaded them, and they were nothing like their original selves. I catch the horse's doleful eye. It catches mine.

What are you doing there, Mr. Murphy? I look. Jesus. It's Mrs. Lewis from the Belnord. I've always liked her and her husband—well-bred, well-heeled, with a spark of mischief in a touch of class. I'm protesting horse-drawn carriages, Mrs. Lewis. I smile up to her. What do you suppose the horses will do when they're free at last, Mr. Murphy? she asks. I hope they'll give us free rides, Mrs. Lewis. I indicate an open space on the sidewalk. Won't you join us? No, Mr. Murphy. She smiles back. I think I'll let you represent our building in the struggle, she says. And off she goes.

By late afternoon, the freeze of the sidewalk has become too much for my fellow civil rightsers. One by one, they up and leave, until only I and a wispy, hair-in-ringlets girl remain. Aren't you cold, sir? she says. I am, I tell her. I hope you won't mind, sir, she says, but I promised my boyfriend I'd meet him at the movies. I hate to leave you all alone. Think nothing of it, I tell her. It was a good demonstration, wasn't it, sir? she says. It sent a message? It's important to send messages, even if no one receives them. Isn't that right, sir? I tell her, It is. We smile to each other as she rises from her squat like a ballerina swan, and glides away. I maintain my place and trace a crack in the sidewalk with my finger. It becomes the bare branch of a tree. I give it leaves.

SAYS HERE THAT "Retirees Flounder with Nothing to Do." Makes you wonder about the retired flounder. What does *he* do, may I ask. Join AARF? Poor fish, he spends a lifetime bent over his subaqueous desk in his airtight cubicle, filling out the same forms, tracing the same flow charts, dining at the same seafood luncheonette, with the same soggy menu, year after year. So at last he retires, and there is nothing ahead but Social Security, Medicare, and swimming swimming swimming. And blowing a few bubbles. Maybe on a Caribbean cruise he'll meet the love of his life, and go to live somewhere near a beach, since he can't go up on the beach, but it's unlikely. Anything good that happens to him from here on out would be a fluke.

Give me a break. "Retirees Flounder with Nothing to Do" but roll around heaven all day? Hmm. Let us address this monumental societal problem, girls and boyos. Whatever can they do? Well, for starters they might sing "What'll I Do" for a year or two. That would be something to do. Or they could sing "Time on My Hands," or more to the point, "What Are You Doing the Rest of Your Life?" You know what Thoreau said—that great old retiree, Thoreau? He said, You can't kill time without injuring eternity. What do you think of that?

Something to do. How about a hobby? Taxidermy? No one talks of taxidermy since Roy and Dale stuffed Trigger, but you don't need to go that big. You can always stuff a flounder. Many have. Speaking of stuffing, how about sticking ships into bottles. Or easier still, placing bottles on ships. How about skeet shooting? Philately? Philandery? Golf? Nothing more exciting than stomping around green places like zombies with sticks in their hands. How about writing a how-to book—*How to Live Old*? I could do that. Make me a *mint*. Yoga parties? Toga parties?

What about fishing itself? If you're going to flounder, after all, why not go for them, too? Retirees of North America, I have an idea. If, at age sixty-five (what wouldn't Murph give to be that again?) you find yourself floundering and asking yourself, what am I doing the rest of my life, here's a thought: live.

YOU DIDN'T KNOW Greenberg but you would have hated him. Everybody did. He was tall as a tree, with eyes like Lawrence of Arabia. (O'Toole's take on Lawrence, anyway. And don't get me started on Peter O'Toole. If every Irishman looked like that, we'd have knocked the bejesus out of the Britons by the year 600.) Yeah, Greenberg was tall and beautiful, and he had hair like an ocean and not a crease or a stain on his happy, open face even when he was well into his sixties. Live? He knew how to live. We were the same age. Strangers took me for his da. And the hated Greenberg went to Yale, where he lettered in lacrosse and baseball, and Harvard Law School, where he was editor of the *Law Review*. He never told me most of this himself. I learned it from friends who hated him as much as I did, and from the other speakers at his memorial service, where I also learned he won the Navy Cross flying choppers over Cambodia. What's worse, he was kind to everyone, and when he made himself rich, he gave his money anonymously to victims of AIDS, wounded vets, war widows, Harlem schools, and to anyone else who needed a hand. His law partners called him Sonny Pro Bono. Did I mention that he played a killer jazz piano, and that he cooked like a chef?

As if that weren't irritating enough, he was great with kids. William worshipped him, and he adored William. I want this, he'd say to me, indicating the boy. A child? I'd ask. No, William, he'd say. Name your price, said Máire.

The time after Oona died, I was sitting the Irish version of shiva, growing a beard, and plastered. Greenberg came over bearing liquid coals to Newcastle, or Coles, to be precise. CDs by Nat and Natalie. Some Blossom Dearie and Linda Ronstadt. Also, a dozen movies. Have I told you about this? Two days, two nights we sat and watched *Dr. Strangelove, Duck Soup, The Horse's Mouth, Kind Hearts and*

Coronets, Morgan, Fletch, The Road to Zanzibar, Caddy Shack,
The Pink Panther, Abbot and Costello Meet Frankenstein, Ani-
mal House, and *Airplane.* Surely you don't know any of these
films, he said as he walked in the house. I know 'em all, I
said. And don't call me Shirley.

What was there not to hate about Greenberg? He
laughed at other people's jokes. He knew when not to say
anything. He knew poetry, came to every one of my readings, with his partner, Barry. It was Barry who killed him,
clubbed Greenberg with the base of a bronze table lamp
as he lay napping. The only thing Barry told the cops was,
He was too good to me. I found his sister Julia's address in
Schenectady, and paid her a call. Greenberg was her only
sibling. She sat on the flowered couch in the three-story
Victorian her brother had bought for her, and served me
tea and cookies. After a silence, Julia said, How could he
die this way? He didn't have an enemy in the world.

ASK ME ABOUT SOULS? I haven't a clue. I believe in them,
but that's as far as I go. It's hard to picture the little buggers. Maybe, once they leave our bodies, they're like flap-
jacks, lying around on plates. Or sponges. Or something
gooey and bouncy like jellyfish. Like gumdrops. Pulsat-
ing like a . . . pulse. Whatever shape they're in, they must
long for the bodies they exited. Don't you think? That's
what they were used to, after all. It creeps me out, actu-

ally, to imagine all the souls of the world flopping around on a beach somewhere, fish out of water. Not a soul in sight but other souls. Heaving with yearning, full of hope and despair, confused, a compound of all we ever were, the essential, fundamental us. Greenberg? Beached? He deserves better.

FIRST THE SEAWEED was dried on the beach, then collected, then loaded on a sorrowful horse and carried somewhere for burning. I watched men do it, and then when I was grown, I did it too. So sad and stupid, the process. So sad and stupid, every process on the island. Collecting the rye straw. Bringing home the straw. Collecting kelp. Bringing home the kelp. A spinning wheel. Threads for a spinning wheel. Harnessing a pony. Threshing. Rope making, so that you could tie the rope to a curragh, tow it out to sea, and die there. Rethatching the roof of a cottage from which, in a year or two, you might be evicted by the Royal Irish Constabulary. If you looked closely at where the thatch was tied to the pegs in the wall, you would make out the different colors—brown, tan, beige, white. Horses' tails in a row. But no one looked closely. No one marveled.

I wondered at the hats of the men, the woolen caps shaped like sagging pancakes. Quirky haberdashery. The poor man's tam-o'-shanter. In their vests and hats the men would pace on the beach with their hands behind their backs, as if they were contemplating issues of great moment. They were not even contemplating issues of small moment. Pacing with their hands behind their backs was just what they did. Animal habit.

They stayed so far away from the women—morning, afternoon, and evening, too, as far as I could tell—it was a miracle that babies ever appeared on Inishmaan. No wonder everyone made such a fuss about praying to the Virgin. I saw it all as a dance in water, figures painted on earthenware. They were candles. They were rumors, made not of fact but rather of implication, tending toward the corner of a whitewashed room, or toward the sea. They had forgotten how to be sad. A life without protest or accusation. A life without vision, guilt, or redemption, slow dancing in the valley of the shadow, flightless, remorseless, at sea.

THE POET'S BUSINESS is to describe everything, but not *everything*. And the everything he does not describe may be as vivid as the everything he does. The space where my da's leg used to be, if you see what I mean. Mark Doty, poet's poet, says as much in his *Art of Description*, when he writes of a morality involved in refusing to describe certain things. He quotes Wisława Szymborska's poem about the people jumping hand in hand from the World Trade Center towers. She shows them in the act of falling, complete, with faces and "blood well hidden," but she will not add "a last line" to her poem, or to their lives. So I too describe what I can of Inishmaan in my poems, but never the faces of the dead. As a boy, I came upon the body of a fisherman washed up on the shore near Allaire's farm. He had on one pampootie, a skin sandal worn by men of the island. A purse remained in his shirt pocket, and he had a box for tobacco in his blue fist. I was alone with the man until the grown-ups arrived, and I saw his face clearly, unclear as it was. That face. But I would never describe it in a poem. The rocks around the body were sufficient. Don't fuck with rocks. They know what they're doing.

> To be a poet is to have a soul so quick to discern, that no shade of quality escapes it, and so quick to feel, that discernment is but a hand playing with finely-ordered variety on the chords of emotion—a soul in which knowledge passes instantaneously into feeling, and feeling flashes back as a new organ of knowledge.
>
> —George Eliot, in Thomas Murphy's
> *Book of Dandy Quotations*

YOU WOULD THINK that going from Inishmaan to Inisheer, a distance of no more than two miles across Foul Sound (can't say we pull punches), would not make much of a voyage. But oh, that night in late October. Sleet sheathed the fields like a caul. The wind was full of rain. It did not let up, rising in wide black sails, and roaring. You oughtn't to have brought the boy, said Will Hargrove to my uncle Jim. I was fourteen. Tommy's strong, said Jim, and a good sailor. That was true. And I wasn't afraid at all, at least not at the start. We lived with wind and rain on the island. And I'd been at sea in a curragh in more storms than I could count.

The tide was supposed to turn at four in the afternoon, but by seven, things had worsened. The wind howled against the rocks. The sea was a battlefield. Pigs ran, and the cows sheltered themselves behind the walls of the houses. I saw a draft horse knocked flat on its side. That's bad luck, said Peter Martins. Others nodded. We were down on the beach with a six-oared boat, surrounding it. Yet it resisted our tugging, as if it were a reluctant old dog and did not want to be dragged out on a night like that. What's the purpose of all this? Peter asked my uncle. We told them we'd be there, said Jim. Can't it wait till morning? said Rory Powers. We promised we'd be there tonight, said Jim.

We tested the braces of the oars and the thole pins. We checked the curragh for leaks. It took the better part of half an hour to drag it from the beach and lift it into the water, the wind pushed so hard against us. One time, the boat reared up like a horse, and Peter Martins called that bad luck too. By the time the six of us had clambered aboard, we were exhausted, and we had not yet started for Inisheer. I rowed in the bow, and I could see nothing ahead of us but the black sea and moonless sky, which were one. Liam Rooney rowed beside me on the thwart. He was older, but slender, and white as a sheet. He said not a word. Not that speaking was easy for anyone. You would hear a shouting, and then the wind would devour it.

I was never so cold, before or since. Soaked through my undershirt and my wool sweater and wool vest, I tried to concentrate on my rowing. If we rode the waves, we'd be all right. But if we were spun around or if we tried to outrun a wave that caught us broadside, we were goners. The curragh leapt and trembled as it went. We leaned into our oars. The bow pitched and wedged into the furrows. Uncle Jim was steering, and he was having a deuce of a time controlling the boat. Two hours out, and the rain had not diminished. If anything, it grew louder and angrier, and the wind carping at the sea.

And then it happened. Starboard, out of the corner of my eye, I caught sight of a massive wave. It seemed to expand as it rushed upon us, high and wide as a house, knocking the curragh on its side, the way the draft horse was knocked. Uncle Jim! I cried. And we tried to right the boat. But the wave had caught us at a right angle, banging the bow so hard it shook like a choking outboard. I held to it for my life, my knuckles frozen on the gunwales. Then I fell on my shoulder, where Liam had been. But Liam was gone.

Dropping my oar, I dived in the water, followed by Will Hargrove and my uncle, while the others remained to hold the boat from capsizing. We were no colder or wetter in the water than out. We called to Liam against the noise of the wind. Liam! Over and over. Liam! There was no human sound in reply. We were clinging to the sides of the curragh, and growing increasingly tired. Liam! Twice I did a surface dive, and saw nothing but the grainy sea, rushing past my eyes. At last we climbed back in, and plunged the boat into the storm again. No one spoke.

Days later, when we returned, I saw Liam's ma pacing on the beach, her head in a shawl. She searched our faces for her son. When my uncle Jim started to walk toward her, she turned away.

BUT TODAY NEW YORK begins in moonlight, and I am glad of it. I smell a wind shift, lifting the grass blades somewhere, skipping over the steppes and surrounding my heart. Shall we blaze in anticipation of the lightning? We tire of the stare of the hypnotized, and begin to glow in several colors. Come with me to the edge of tears. Beautiful, is it not? The candle gutters but stays lit, casting a shield of light over the blue fields and the blue ice of the Chrysler Building, and the throbbing sea between them.

Let the beasts stomp in their stalls. Let the ladies paint their toenails scarlet. Muster the troops. We have places to get to, now that the streets are cleared of snow. You never crash if you go full tilt. Brown penny. My head bursts with flowers.

AND TODAY IS Máire's fortieth birthday, too, which she hates my mentioning, thinking that at forty she's over the hill. And we're together at Gunn's, a half restaurant, half bar, all-Irish dive where the customers sing their hearts out at the drop of a hat. I don't mean karaoke. That's too modern and too easy for Gunn's. The folks who come here are as old as I am, or young people with old souls, and they know the words to all the songs they want to sing. The piano player at the chipped and scarred and tinny upright is Rory, a guy my age, who, they say, was left in a basket at Gunn's and decided never to leave. Rory plays everything in the key of C. It's the only key he knows. Still, when anyone asks him to play this or that, he always asks, What key? The person says F-sharp. Rory nods, and plays it in C.

Rory! I call from our table. Máire cringes, attempting to disappear beneath her hands clasped over her head. Do you know "Happy Birthday to You"? I ask him. I want to serenade my daughter. Why? he says. Don't you like her? In B-flat major minor, I say to him. Maestro, if you please?

Right! shouts Rory, And I belt out "Happy Birthday" in the key of C, quite beautifully, if I say so myself, and there's not a damp eye in the house. Everyone joins in, and blushing Máire is obliged to stand and curtsy. What a beauty! shouts Rory from the piano bench. Am I not! I say. And the whole place boos.

What'd you get me for my birthday, Murph? She puts on her little girl Christmas face. I got you this necklace, I say, reaching into my pocket and displaying a string of antique pearls set in a purple velvet case. Her eyes widen. They belonged to your mother, I say. They did? she says, then searches my expression. She always knows when I'm lying. No, they didn't, she says. Well, I say, they belonged to somebody's mother. Anyway, they're beautiful, she says. Thank you, Murph.

I also wrote a poem for you. Oh! Read it, Murph? Don't mind if I do, I say, and take out my little notepad.

> Of all the fauna and the flora
> No one's as lovely as my Máire.

Oh, Jesus! she says.

> Lovely at twenty, lovely at thirty
> Lovely when she's talking dirty.

May I go home now? She pretends to reach for her coat.

> Lovely at thirty-five, lovely at thirty-nine,
> Lovely drinking beer, ale, whiskey, or wine.

She sticks her thumb down her throat, as if trying to gag.

> Lovely if you call her Shorty . . .

Oh no, you don't, she says. Don't you dare.

> Lovely still, at the ripe old age of . . .

She drops her napkin in my drink.

I don't know what you're complaining about, I tell her. You're a spring chicken. It's me who's old. You're telling me, she says. Old, wicked, drooling. I'm not drooling, I protest. And with all that, I say, you have to admit that I'm the cutest seventy-two-year-old you ever saw. True, she says. You're cute the way otters are cute. Cute face, mean spirit. I wouldn't mind being an otter, I say. Lie on your back all day, eating and dreaming. So different from your own life, says my ungrateful child.

Otter dreams, I say. What do you suppose an otter dreams about? Besides herring? says Máire. Maybe learning to swim on its tummy. I brighten at her idea. Let's write a children's book, I suggest. *The Otter Who Learns the Breaststroke.* How would the book begin? she says. I lean over the table toward her. One day, I say in my best children's book tone, the sweetest, prettiest, smartest lady otter in all the world, woke up, stretched at the sunlight, and exclaimed, It's my birthday! Shit! I'm forty! Máire has her Irish up now. You are going to get it, she says, rising from her chair. Time to tickle the world's oldest, meanest otter.

She knows I can't stand to be tickled. I rise from my chair at once, and move away from her around the table, Máire in hot pursuit. Still circling, I call to Rory, "Happy Birthday" one more time, me boy? What key? he asks. Becky Sharp flat Asia minor, I tell him. You bet! says Rory, hitting a major chord in middle C. And once more the entire joint bursts out singing "Happy Birthday to You" to my beloved daughter, who stands in surrender with her arms at her sides, and helplessly laughs.

DO YOU BELIEVE in unsaid things? She takes my arm as we walk together in the littered park across the street from her house. She phoned me on her own, because she wants to talk without Jack around. It's been a while since my dinner at their house, and I am beginning to hope that I was out of a job, that Jack had mounted the courage to tell her his fatal news without my help. Unsaid things, Murph. Do you believe in them?

I deal in things unsaid, Sarah. It's my meat.

You do, yes. But you say them, if you see what I mean. You write them. And as soon as you do, they're no longer unsaid. I'm talking about the things no one says, ever. Not poets. Not anyone.

Then how would we know they exist? I ask her. By unsaid do you also mean unthought?

Yes. Unthought. Or maybe unused. A realm of reality that lives between the nodes of reality.

What do you have in mind, Sarah? You're troubled by something. Yes?

I'm troubled by lots of things, Murph. By sightlessness. By Jack. I know he wants to tell me he's dying. Or he wants you to tell me, so that you or he will feel you did the right thing.

The right thing?

The kind thing, she says. Kindness is often one of the unsaid things.

Sarah? I study her composure. She is wearing a light raincoat and a bright red-and-yellow scarf. I ask her, Should I apologize that Jack and I plotted to tell you his diagnosis?

Never, she says, patting my arm. But it makes me feel more alone, more lonely. The worst part of being blind, Murph, is the loneliness, you know. She takes a few more steps deliberately, as if she were timing what she would say next. No, I don't mind the plotting. What I mind is that it isn't true.

What isn't true?

Jack isn't dying, Murph. He isn't even sick. She turns her head to me. He has someone else. He's had someone else for shy of a year. He wants to leave me and go live with her. But he knows he can't walk out on a blind wife. He wants me to think he's dying, so I'll forgive him his trespasses. You're just part of a larger story, a scam, in which he will say something like he needs to go and die alone, like an elephant. I'll be in mourning and he'll be off with Brunhilde, or whatever her name is. I really don't know what he has in mind. He's out of control, not used to dealing in a world of conflicted emotions, so he comes up with a wild plan involving you.

She says all this without a single gulp or change of inflection, in a voice neither calm nor angry, more like someone announcing a bus schedule.

Jack has found someone else, Murph. It happens. He doesn't know how to express his feelings about it. Fact is, he doesn't know how to express his feelings for her, or for me, which he thinks amounts to a betrayal of me. And, in a way, it does. But they are perfectly reasonable feelings for someone in love, even though he's no longer in love with me. Yet he still loves me. Habit? He's flailing. You were caught in the flail. He doesn't know what to call what he's feeling and neither do I. No one does. Right, Murph? Which is why I asked you if you believed in unsaid things.

I WISH I COULD tell you that this was the first time I'd
been snookered, but it happens all the time. It may be
me, the way I was made. Máire detected it right off. Most
daughters do, when it comes to dads. They say that every
girl child, as soon as she is born, looks up through the film
on her eyes, sees her father and thinks, Sucker. I overplay
the part. Or it may have some connection with being a
poet—the sort of willed innocence we boyos use to regard
everything, no matter how often we have seen it, as a wonder, a bright miracle. Still, I'd never been snookered the
way Jack did it to me. A cold-blooded piece of work in the
first place, telling someone you're dying when you're not.
And then making me his unwitting coconspirator in the
hoodwinking of his blind wife, just so he could run off
with some doxie. Jesus, Mary, and What's-his-name.

So I set out to find old Jack, to give him a piece of my
mind, which in my state of mental health was a risky
donation. But At Swim-Two-Birds is the only place I knew
to look, and no one had seen him there. Jimmy doesn't
even remember him, which makes me wonder if Jack
had been in the bar just that one day, specifically to find
me. It hardly takes a Sherlock Holmes to figure out where
Murph does his drinking. It occurs to me—too late, of
course—that I do not know what Jack does for a living, or
where he works. I consider asking Sarah, but there was
something about the melancholy cool, the profound resignation with which she had told me what Jack was up to,

that suggested I leave her be. She had wanted to be up front with me, so that I wouldn't be implicated in Jack's lie. It was a decent thing to do.

With no choice but to cool my heels, I do just that. And the Jack and Sarah affair is supplanted by things in my control. William and I have our next Central Park adventure, that turns into a near-disaster, something I want to forget, and I don't say that often. Dr. Spector schedules me for a brain scan. I try to put it off by claiming that my scurvy is acting up again, also my rickets, but Máire says she's going to march me over to the scan herself. I work on the poem to Oona, but it is getting away from me. Sometimes that happens with a poem. You start out writing tight, and then you overthink the thing, and it gets bigger and bigger without getting better. I plan various ways of eliminating Perachik, such as planting a bomb in his Mets cap. But it might not kill him.

Then one afternoon Sarah calls, her voice uncharacteristically shaky. Jack's disappeared. She has not seen him since the day she and I had our walk in the park. I ask all the predictable questions about who might know where he is. His family? His boss? There is no family, far as she knows. And, strange to report, she knows next to nothing about Jack's employment, except that he's a bouncer in some club in New Jersey. She doesn't even know what city. Now that she thinks about it, the club could be in Pennsylvania, or Delaware, or upstate, some town near the

Hudson. I realize how odd this sounds, she says. But Jack always was evasive about his work, because he thought I'd look down on it, whereas you know, Murph, I don't look down or up at anything. Her attempt to leaven the matter.

Have you called the cops? I ask her. They told her that Jack could not be considered a missing person officially unless she came to the stationhouse and made a formal report. When told of her condition, a lieutenant offered to come to her place but advised her to wait a few more days. In his experience with these matters, he said, husbands and wives come and go. That was a few days ago. Now I'm scared, Sarah says. Otherwise, I wouldn't have bothered you, Murph. Fact is, we don't have many friends, Jack and I. And the few we have I wouldn't turn to. My folks are useless snobs. They'll be glad that Jack's gone. When I ask her, why turn to me, she says she thinks I'm someone she can trust. And she's right, I guess. Only, I see that instead of being a casual visitor to Sarah's isolated world, I'm becoming a key player. I'm not sure I like this role. Would you? Connections with strangers means connections with strangers.

THEN AGAIN, what do I know of Jack? Sarah says he doesn't know himself. Does anyone? Yeats congratulated Synge for writing of Aran, and expressing "a life that never found expression." What life anywhere has found expression? The true life, I mean, if there is such a thing. The island I was born on is no more hidden than the island I live on now. What do we know? What do we ever know?

In my thirties, I knew a writer named Harkness who was so hail-fellow, so welcoming and exuberant that you were made glad just to see his smiling face. The kind of guy you want to catch sight of when you walk into a crowded bar, and his hand shoots up when he sees you—Hey, Murph!—and he beckons you to join a gang of strangers to whom he introduces you all 'round, and makes you feel as if you belong. That sort of guy.

So one day out of the blue, Harkness disappears from the scene. Poof. Without a by-your-leave he packs a few clothes and takes off from his apartment on St. Marks Place for the island of St. Martin, where he gets a job washing dishes in a dive near the docks. He leaves his writing behind, and his books, not to mention a wife of longstanding and two kids under ten. Now, this is the kindest guy in the world, I'll remind you. He once gave his whole book advance to the daughter of someone he hardly knew, so that she could go to Juilliard. And it wasn't as if he had money to burn, either. 'Twas just the way he was. Anyway, off he goes to wash dishes in St. Martin, and live in a ramshackle room above a tobacco store. No words of explanation to anyone. His wife follows him down there, and he greets her warmly and calmly and says he's never coming back. Friends visit him from time to time, and he gives them the same treatment. No number of pleas can make a dent. He's where he wants to be, he says.

Then one day, he wants to be somewhere else. His fellow workers in the dive report that just after sunup one morning, Harkness takes out a skiff and points it toward the deep Caribbean, never to return. Assumed drowned. I am telling you, there was no one on Earth better with people than Harkness. Yet on one vague tropical morning, he does without anyone. The outgoing Harkness goes out forever. What do we know? What do we ever know? People with dementia: Do they know who they were?

OR ARE YOU WONDERING if I'm dreaming all this up? The way I dream up? Think about it, you say to yourself. We're getting the whole story from Murph. No one else remembers seeing Jack but Murph, not even the bartender Jimmy. Just like old Murph. The cockamamie tale of Jack and Sarah? Wise Sarah and unfaithful Jack? Oh, and Sarah's blind. That's a nice touch. The old crock is talking through his hat. Or worse, he really is bonkers, just as Máire fears, and he doesn't know when something is happening or when he's shooting the breeze. The estimable Dr. Spector said as much. He is as capable of forgetting what did not occur as he is of forgetting the eggs.

Well, what can I tell you? I'm on your side. The whole thing sounds like horseshit. But there they were, nonetheless, the two of them. Or rather, the one of them, since Jack has flown the coop. There they were, in their tidy little Queens house, with their lies and their troubled marriage, and me in the middle, as well as the muddle. And as for the possibility that I'm remembering something that never happened, isn't that nearly always the case? You think you remember this and that, but you don't. You get it wrong. It wasn't a Tuesday, it was Thursday. It wasn't 2010. It was 1986. And she was left-handed, not right. And she wasn't a she. But you believe in the memory anyway. Your childhood. Your parents. Your teachers. Your pals. Your lovers. Yourself. Your brave, cowardly, sensitive, senseless, adventurous, terrified self. You don't have an accurate thought in your head, about you or anyone or anything in this holy mess of a life. But you believe you do. Memory is belief, a kind of faith. You have to dream it up. Otherwise you have no past to cling to. Right? You know I'm right.

HERE'S MY GRIPE about forgetfulness. Not that you asked. My gripe is that not enough is said about the beauty of it, the wondrous, glorious loveliness of not remembering what you want to remember, or are supposed to remember. I mean, overcook a few eggs, and your daughter calls the booby hatch. Or visit your publisher Hornby's house in Mamaroneck, and stroll into his swimming pool when you're still wearing your jacket and slacks, because you're daydreaming, and everyone is ready to strap on the straitjacket. Either they deem it a sin or a social crime, forgetfulness.

But think of the fullness in forgetfulness—the universe of thought and feeling that forgetfulness replaces for the things forgotten. Or the people. Or the incidents. I think there's a high selectivity that goes on in the brain, imaginatively choosing things we get wrong over things we get right. Words forgotten can be a pain. But the process of foraging for those words can be thrilling, like foraging for the right word in a line of a poem. The wrong word is wrong, to be sure. Still, it can be a beauty. A voyage. An obscenity.

And incidents forgotten may be preferable to incidents remembered. You forget something that happened to you because it simply is too painful, like my da's dying. The mother of a friend of mine has Alzheimer's. She is eighty-six today. As a teenage girl she survived Auschwitz, the beatings and the rapes. Now, she has forgotten about everything, including Auschwitz. My friend says, with a saddened satisfaction, See? She has beaten the Nazis twice.

And then there are incidents that never happened in the first place, ones you have made up whole cloth. You forget they never happened. You invented them because, for some shadowy reason, you needed them. You can get all bound up in them, carrying them to ridiculous lengths, because you wish that they had happened even though they hadn't. It is pleasing, maybe rescuing, for you to think they happened. But they never did, and you forget.

I probably forget a good deal more than I let on to you or to Máire or Dr. Spector. But those forgotten things, though they remain forgotten, have a life of their own. Don't you think? And a place of their own, too. They live somewhere else, like the world's not. They live in dreams. Professor Dodds has a chapter on Homer in which he writes of the early Greeks who believed so ardently in dreams, they saw themselves as living in two worlds at once—real life and dream life. Dual citizenship. The things we forget are no matter. They are another matter. Another kettle of eggs. A vine may grow out of a ship's plank. Who would doubt it? You can sink your teeth into an idea like that, if sinking your teeth floats your curragh, because as any good Dionysian votary knows, time and space and their attending horseshit do not exist in the world's not. And if everyone is lonely in the world, then it goes without saying that no one is lonely in the world's not. Makes sense. No? Or nonsense.

Let us hie thither, that's what I say. Let us go nowhere. There's beauty there, I'm sure of it. Or not. That's the thing about nowhere. Everything forgotten exists and does not in the world's not, world without end, or not. No end. Not not. Not you, not I. And if we look carefully enough, or carelessly as it were, or were not, we should find no meaning there. None. And wouldn't *that* be nothing!

THEN SHE WANDERED into McCraken's field at four in the morning, hiked up her flannel nightie, and peed on a rock. Then she called me by Pa's name. Then she caressed a shirt drying on the line, and when I said, Ma, what are you doing, she told me to hush, it was none of my business. Then she cursed a jackdaw in language so vile, I thought at first that she was gagging on a bone. There followed a long period of silence, followed by a period of equal duration in which she told me how a boy named Niall had loved her when she was in school, and how he wanted to marry her and take her to raise sheep in New Zealand. But he was so short, Tommy. Sweet but very short. You have to eat something, Ma, I said. Then she ate a little, and less each day. Then she stopped and had to be fed through a tube. Then she was clear as a bell for a couple of weeks, and I asked the doctor if she was coming back. No, he said. These spates of clarity are part of the progress of the disease. She will return to her darkness, soon, he said. And she did. And I wondered—in the times she was silent, or sleeping, or reviling the Jamaican nurse I'd got her from the mainland, or singing the wrong words to the wrong tune—if all that were kind of a terrible mask, and the woman wearing the mask, under the mask, was lucid, right as rain, with a mind as smart and pure as it had been before all this started. I wondered if that imprisoned mind was confused and frustrated at the things the mask was saying in her behalf, yet could do nothing to remove the mask. Was she, in other words, my ma? Then I found her poring over a book. Then I saw she had ripped out the pages.

SUCH A (what do they call it?) learning experience, poring over *The Atlas of the World* with William. Is this a country or a city, Murph? What do you think, William? I think it's an elephant. It looks like Elephantus, Murph! William! What would Elephantus be doing in an atlas? What does Elephantus do *anywhere*, Murph? Flops around. Jumps around. Ah, that's where I've got you, my boyo. Elephants can't jump. Wow! I never knew that, Murph. You know everything! Where's Ireland? Here? No. That's Africa. Is Ireland in Africa? I don't think so. Is Africa in Ireland? Definitely. The little hand flips the pages. What's this island, Murph? That's Devil's Island, William. Also known as England. Does the devil live there? Millions of 'em, I tell him. There's a garden in this country, Murph. He points to Mozambique. How do you know, William? I can smell the bees, he says, in all seriousness. Well, William, you know what Gibbon said. Who's Gibbon, Murph? Gibbon said education is lost on everyone except happy

people, who don't need it anyway. Is that Ireland, Murph?
Peru, William. Close enough.

THEY SAY THAT Irishmen drink to forget we're Irish. I
say we drink to remember we're Irish, because our poor
dismal history consists of English swine trying to kick
the Irish out of us. We set up the hedge schools as a show
of our determination to teach the Irish language. No one
really wanted to learn it. Irish is a limited language, truth
be told, especially for modern poetry, though there's a
sweet sound of whispers to it. No, the hedge schools were
simply another way to stick it to the Brits. It takes a jar
or three to remind an Irishman that he has a culture, a
nation, a sound.

Want to know why the Irish make good poets? Sure you
do. You're dying to know. Well, we make good poets because
we know how to deal in absent things, the things taken
from our lives, like food and dignity. And legs. We've been
learning to do without since the ancient Irish writings left
out vowels. No vowels in ancient Irish. Try pronouncing a
sentence of that. Then again, the spoken language of today
adds more words when you expect less, too, just to prove
our English is different. There is no word for *yes* or *no* in
Irish and none in our use of English either. Ask an Irish
woman if it's cold outside, she'll say, "It is." Ask an Irishman if he's happy, he'll say, "I am." I take that back. No

Irishman is happy. But you get the point. We stretch out the sentences. I mean, what the hell else do we have to do but talk?

Now I'm not including Kerrymen in all this because Kerry is the stupidest county in Ireland by miles, which is saying something, since all the counties in Ireland compete for the title of stupidest. But Kerrymen are also unique in that they only answer a question with a question. This proposition was put to the test one day when a visitor to the county stood directly across the street from the post office, and asked a Kerryman passing by if that was the post office over there. The Kerryman looked and said, Is it a letter you'd be mailin'? And they can be sharp when it suits them. At a Kerry funeral, someone was asked to say a few kind words about the deceased, who was hated by the whole town. The eulogist said, His brother was worse.

Synge, my fellow Inishmaan resident, was more typically Irish than most of our writers, even though he was a Protestant, or a West Brit as we like to call 'em. But in his cramped rented room in the cottage on Inishmaan, called Synge's Cottage today, he listened well to the talk going on in the kitchen. And because he had an ear for music, he picked up the rhythms of the talk for his dialogues. More than that, he caught the essence of the country, the beauty and the madness—how a blind couple could love and hate each other in *The Well of the Saints,* how a town could make a hero of a boy who boasted that he'd killed his da, in *The Playboy of the Western World,* and how an old man could break his heart over a young woman in love with a young man, and how all could be brought down in *Deirdre of the Sorrows.* Synge, who was dying when he wrote *Deirdre,* was in love with a much younger woman himself, the knockout actress Molly Allgood. He wrote a poem predicting how she would react to those who bore his casket, that she would rend them with her teeth.

On the island Synge used to sit in a stone seat now called Synge's Chair. Have I told you about this? Just messin' with you.

Rend. Teeth. Lovely words. *Penny, brown penny.* Lovely words. *Oona* was a lovely word. *Greenberg* was a lovely word. What happens to a person when the words go, do you suppose? And how do they go—in clusters, or one by one, like the lethal computer Hal in *2001,* whose vocabulary dwindled to a precious few words after Keir Dullea pulled his plug? I don't recall Hal's very last words. What will be mine? I wonder. Something profound and ethereal, like Goethe's "More light"? Maybe "More lite beer."

THOMAS JAMES MURPHY, the celebrated poet, genius, cardsharp, pop singer, piano bar player, raconteur, bon vivant, and all-around good guy died last night in his home in New York City, from complications arising from a loss of memory. His daughter, Máire, reports that for the past few months Mr. Murphy had been wondering which of two forms of death—of the body or the mind—would take him first. As it turned out, both forms reached him simultaneously. He forgot to go on living. Born on Inishmaan in the Aran Islands, Mr. Murphy, who was devilishly handsome, with a joie de vivre and a coupe de ville and his heavenly baritone voice and sea-blue eyes, sailed to New York in his early twenties, and at once established himself as a literary wunderkind. Lillian Hellman herself knew him as Timothy. And he never wrote back to W. D. Snodgrass. Critics hailed his work as astonishingly original, amazingly derivative, delightful, repellant, hard-edged, mawkish, brilliant, and stupid. His wife of fifty years, the former Oona O'Donnell, died of endometrial cancer, a year ago in January. It was said that "Murph," as he was known, was never the same afterward, which most of his friends regarded as an improvement. Beside his perfect if pain-in-the-ass daughter, Mr. Murphy is survived by his delicious grandson, William, Jimmy the gabby publican, Jameson Distillers, by his new friend Sarah, and by the superintendent of his apartment house, Danny Perachik, a known rat. Mr. Murphy's last words were . . . I forget.

FROM THE FAR SIDE of her desk, that rises like the Great Wall of China, Dr. Spector regards me as if I were a can of spoiled sardines. In return I give her my cutest smile, which seems to further displease her. I know you're used to people being charmed by you, Mr. Murphy, she says, and I'm sure you thought I'd be tickled pink by your answers to the Ohio State test I sent you home with. I start to say I didn't know what color she'd be tickled, but she goes on. Mr. Murphy, I'm going to treat you like a grown-up. A stretch, I realize. But you have been wasting my time. And hard as it may be to believe, my time is valuable. Every second I devote to your nonsense, I take away from someone who wants and deserves to be helped.

You're also wasting your own time, she says, and there may not be much of that left. Your daughter tells me the super in your building reports that you've left your front door wide open at least half a dozen times in the past weeks. (I must remember to cut out Perachik's liver.) That's in addition to the now myth-size eggs and swimming pool stories. She says you're also starting to make things up that could not have occurred, but you seem to believe them. (I meant to tell you about the front door business, but it slipped my mind.)

So, these are signs, Mr. Murphy. I can't say how bad, but definitely heading downward. I start to speak, but she shuts me up with a wave of her hand. I am finding her less like Joanne Woodward by the second, and more like Judith Anderson in *Rebecca,* without Judith's puckish sense of humor.

Let me tell you what we're dealing with here, scientifically, Mr. Murphy. Memory is a tricky item. It resides in patterns of neural activity all throughout the brain. After "neural activity" I begin to tune her out. There follows science shit, followed by more science shit at "cortex," followed by "FDA-approved drugs," followed by two more references to science shit, followed by "fiber tracks," followed by "schedule a brain scan for you," followed by science shit, science shit, and science shit. Our one-sided colloquy concludes with, But until then, Mr. Murphy, I want you to shape up. And before you fall to your knees and assure me of your heartwarming reformation, since I don't trust you, I'm going to inform your daughter of everything I've told you today. In short, you're cooked, Mr. Murphy. She exits before I can ask her for a balloon.

THE PARK IS GRAY and I am blue, thinking about how long it takes to live a life, and what do you wind up with? Age. People say it's unseemly to feel sorry for yourself, but I enjoy feeling sorry for myself. Who else would feel sorry for me? It gives me a hole to crawl out of when I write my poems. Snap out of it, Murph, I say. And then I do. Oona used to say it for me. I hear her now. Snap out of it, Murph. I keep walking and try. September is New York's best month, don't you think? You feel the sunshine and the shrinkage all at once. Accordion days. Too bad it's January.

Three teenage girls sidle past me on the walking path. Two Irish, one Italian is my guess, each of them pretty and smiling and nodding to the old man. Snodgrass again: younger, pinker, out of reach. I smile back, like a dead star. I proceed a few steps and feel a hard shot to the nape of my neck. Now I'm down on my back in the path with the three darling teenage tree nymphs whom I passed a couple of seconds ago standing over me, and telling me to give them my money. See these? says the tall brunette, holding up the back of her hand and indicating her fingernails filed sharp as lobster forks. I'll cut you with these. Then the plump blonde kicks me square in the ribs. The stash, she says. They still use that word?

I reach under me for my back pocket and my wallet, and present all I have, maybe a hundred. That seems to drive the girls wild with happiness. The third girl, with the tattooed throat, gives me one more shot in the thigh for good measure before they all run off shouting and hooting. I'd have kicked their asses if I'd had four other guys with me.

Limping home from the park, I spot the sometimes-poet Arthur again. Arthur! Murph! Arthur the Bear! Murph the Bard! Today his mood is up. He has established an outdoor living room in front of the church on Amsterdam and Eighty-sixth. Apparently he has scavenged furnishings from the local garbage, and has come up with a fairly complete place, consisting of a maroon sofa, with frayed floral-pattern upholstery, a Barcalounger with a missing arm, a couple of deck chairs, two unmatching end tables bearing two porcelain lamps plugged into nothing, and a three-legged plastic coffee table resting on an orange shag rug. I enter his room, and take one of the deck chairs. Arthur sits on his sofa, as always bundled against the cold, and looking more bearlike than ever, but otherwise at ease and self-possessed.

I just got mugged in the park, Arthur, I tell him. That's nothing, Murph. When I'm living in my cave, I get mugged all the time. Well, maybe you're right, I say. I'm probably making too much of it. How's tricks, Arthur? Good, Murph. Good. Couldn't be better. He hesitates. I want to remain with him in case the cops come, so I can explain his condition to them. But I'm kind of busy just now, he says. We sit in silence for a minute. He grumbles. Writing any poems? I ask. He shakes his massive head. I get the feeling I'm boring him. He stares at me impatiently. Finally, he says, I don't mean to be rude, Murph. But I'm expecting guests.

DEAR MURPH,

I like good singing as much as the next guy. And I don't have to tell you, you have great pipes. But when you stand in the courtyard at midnight, belting out

"What Are You Doing the Rest of Your Life?" at the
top of your lungs, all four verses, the people in the
building complain. And I mean loud complaints.
About twenty of them. So, please, Murph. No more. I
wouldn't want to have to report this to the landlord.

    Yours sincerely,
    Daniel A. Perachik (Dan)
    Superintendent

    P.S. It didn't help that you were singing in your
skivvies.

Dear Danny Boy,
    May I drop over and strangle you?
    Yours sincerely,
    Thomas J. Murphy
    Strangler

IF MCCLEERY CAN DO IT, I can do it. Have I told you about
this? About McCleery? He strangled a dog. Big mother, it
growled at McCleery and bared its teeth. And McCleery
strangled it with his hands. Picked it up by the throat,
stared straight into its wild red eyes, and choked the life
out of it. Right there, in his own backyard. A cart wobbled
down the road, drawn by a donkey covered in mud. An owl
wheeled under the moon. Mrs. McCleery told her sister

from Wicklow to get out of the kitchen, and stay out. And McCleery strangled a dog.

KNOW WHAT I THINK? Of course you do. I'm always telling you what I think. I think these people, Dr. Spector and her crew of experts, have a severely limited view of memory. Some years ago, I was giving a reading at a college in Ohio, in the science building, of all places. And on the way to the auditorium, I walked past this massive wall chart of the human genome that tracked our genetic makeup back millions of years, to the chimps. So I asked a biologist who taught at the college how much of what people are made up of today existed in the original chimps. She said 95 percent. See what I mean? Our bodies are memory. The whole human race is composed of memory. My point is you can't lose your memory. You can misplace it, or relocate it. But you can't lose it, no matter what Máire or Dr. Spector or Perachik the informer says, unless your definition of memory is as narrow as an open door or a swimming pool or a fucking egg. Who cares if I forget my area code, for Chrissake? And the only reason I strolled into Hornby's pool was that I get so flummoxed in social situations, I put myself in a daze. I could have walked anywhere. Lucky he doesn't live in a penthouse.

About Perachik? How am I or anyone to know if what he's saying about me is true? The little rat has a vested interest in getting me out of the Belnord, and into some assisted nuthouse. My landlord, to whom Perachik would not want to have to report my behavior, would pay the honorable superintendent a handsome little squealer's fee for services rendered to get his greedy paws on my rent-stabilized eleven rooms, and make three apartments out of them, each renting for five times what I pay now for the whole shebang. Why would anyone base an opinion of anything on the word of the slimy bastard, Perachik, I'd like to know. And there are only three verses to "What Are You Doing the Rest of Your Life?" Just sayin'.

All right, all right. Dr. Spector has a point. If my behavior keeps spiraling down, I'll be a fucking albatross to Máire and William. So when that happens, I'll know it, I'm certain of that. And I'll go to Virginia or some other enlightened state where a Dalmatian puppy can pick up a shotgun at a fruit stand, and I won't forget the shells, and I'll blow my empty head off. But until that time, let me glory in the fact that I am memory, and you are memory, and you can think about that next time you crave a banana.

SO I CALL OUT to the boyos carrying the curragh on Eighty-sixth Street outside the Belnord, Where are you going with that? We're goin' fishin', old man. Want to come? You bet! I say. And we head through the park over to the East River, toss the curragh in the water, and jump in after. It's a hell of a town, New York, is it not? I say. 'Tis, they say. They got girls here and fish and poems, too. What else do you need? Not a goddam thing, we all agree. And we're drinking pints and singing songs and having a grand old time, until a yacht comes along and wakes us, and we drown.

HAD I NOT been asleep, William, I would have missed the otters.

What otters, Murph?

The otters who were marching in my dream, William.

Were they soldiers, Murph?

They were. But they were soldiers without guns. They had bananas instead. And when they had finished with their marching, they laid down their bananas, and went swimming on their backs, the way otters do. Otters are masters of the backstroke, William. Your mother loves them. Ask her.

Are otters friendly, Murph?

Very. They also look you in the eye. I never met a shifty otter. They also read the classics. Like *War and Otters* and *The Otter Also Rises*. A great author named Homer wrote a long poem called the *Ottersy*, about a brave hero named Otterseus. Otters have a wonderful life. They lie on their backs, balance books on their tummies, and read the day away.

I wish I could see them.

Well, if you fall asleep now, right now, you might see them. If you don't fall asleep, you might miss them. What's worse, William [kissing his forehead, and pulling up his covers], the otters will miss you.

Night, Murph.

Night, my boy.

A LETTER from Sarah:

Dear Murph, I hope you won't mind my writing you. But with Jack gone—I did file a missing person's report—I have no companionship. And writing affords companionship, as I don't need to tell you. Let me be clear, though, before you get all anxious and think, Oh Jesus, do I have to become this blind girl's pen pal? Or worse, exchange opinions on books with her, like those stories of high-minded, like-minded literary poo-bahs? Not at all. In fact, Murph, I'd prefer that you do not write back. For one thing, I don't want you to go to the trouble of making tapes or CDs, or even more difficult, using one of those gizmos that type braille. (I'm using a braille typewriter myself, a Perkins Brailler, which is great but a pain in the ass.)

     It's not worth the effort. I'm not worth the effort. You would reach this conclusion yourself after not too long a while, and you would resent me, which I do not want. Mainly, I just want to be able to call out to you once in a while, as a second conscience. Think of these letters as messages without a return address. Does that make sense? If I knew I was writing them only to myself, there would be no pleasure in it. It would exacerbate my loneliness, not relieve it. But if I know you're at the receiving end, Murph, I can spill my guts, such as they are, and know you'll catch what I'm tossing. (A revolting image.) In any case, thanks in advance, as they say. More anon, as they also say. Who are these "they," anyway? And why aren't they around when you need them? As ever, Sarah.

UNDER THE WHITE COVERLID, now as then, my Belnord cottage rolls, the same cool turning. Memories run wild, as if the night had released all its prisoners. My ghosts are younger now. Imagine that. I am older than my ghosts, yet they retain a certain je ne sais quoi—authority? I love this time of night, this bed that makes me alert to everything— the hours, the planes in flight, the faucet drip. My senses gleam like candles. Sleep with me, life. There is no break- age, no estrangement. Fuck dementia.

REMEMBER THE DREAMS instead. Remember, for instance, the morning Mannahatta first came into view, through a gauze so dense, you could not tell if the magic isle was in front of your nose or elsewhere, miles away. And the fact that the immense island floated on geysers of air did not help. It swayed this way and that, and also that way, sometimes quavering like an arthritic hand, sometimes soaring starward, yet without rising. The density was noteworthy—five hundred feet of adamant, layered over with strata of minerals and topsoil, the muck and oozings of the land from which vertical rocks rose, archives blazing in the suns. There were two suns, one above the island, no more than three hundred feet high, one below at the same remove. Infinity glimmering. What a sight for a boyo from the Emerald Isle, who had not laid eyes on an emerald in all his twenty years. But Mannahatta was agog with emeralds and sapphires and rubies, diamonds too. Oh, the diamonds! Bracelets and tiaras encircling the flagpoles.

Drawing near, one could see that the island sloped downward in a funnel toward the center, where thousands of wide clay pots, vats really, collected rainwater and converted it into books. Flagons of mead were distributed to the poor, who (foolishly) used them as bocci balls. A prelate banged a crozier on a marble table. A baker paled. Along the walls of the slope were staircases consisting of thousands of steps from which people fished for carp and compliments. Guidebooks told that the principal occupations of Manhattanites were music, mathematics,

and butchering, and that the women were rich and loose.
Nearer still, and it seemed that the staircases were made
of bone. Alabaster, perhaps. Or snow.

At the center of the water vats, there appeared to be a
black hole or chasm, that upon closer inspection turned
out to be a bazaar, as in the *Arabian Nights*, the booths con-
structed out of the wrecks of ships, like ours, ships from
all over the world that had sailed to Mannahatta for centuries. The booths displayed china dogs and precious rugs
and fabrics—bolts of red and gold cloth, and works of art,
both fine and cheap, and slaves, too, both black and white,
whose singing talent was evident even at our distance, and
whose chains dazzled in the light. A perpetual thunder-
storm roiled therein, and gulped and gasped, its noise so
deafening we plugged our ears. The rain licked the cob-
blestones on the quays.

Stone-eyed kids ran to greet us at the pier, ragged and
scrawny, in pleated skirts and prep school blazers with
coats of arms. They wore garlands of green leaves and sang
in a language none of us knew. A bier bearing the body of
an ancient priest with a thick white beard was wheeled in
among them, and hundreds of the citizens lined up to view
it. Some identified the man as their father. Others did not.
At the appearance of the bier, the children dispersed, and
then the bier disappeared. Where the bazaar had stood
only moments earlier, there now was a flat grassy plain,
with a few scattered pedestals in disrepair, and stone

heads fallen at the bases, as in a defunct outdoor sculpture gallery. Excitement rolled through our decks, first class to steerage, but just as we were about to tie up at the pier, the immense island lurched and flew again, making it impossible for us to reach it. Then the stone-eyed kids returned and tossed us ropes. And at last we were home. Remember?

SELF-MADE EXILES like me are a dime a dozen, and that goes for fussy, cock-o'-the-walk Jimmy Joyce as well. Pray silence for the gates, the ones who remain in the fields, swinging open and closed, coming nowhere, going nowhere. Hinged, unhinged. A tip of the cap to those who stay put, the grayed deadwood not fit for kindling. The gates. The gates are Ireland.

SAYS HERE IN "Why Do Men Love Islands?" that Masafumi Nagasaki, a seventy-six-year-old skinny boyo with a nice even tan (the photo), lives in hermetic solitude and "apparently content" on a rocky island off the Japanese coast. Way to go, Masafumi. Says your island is "inhospitable," and that you have endured typhoons, as you walk around naked. Glad they have no photo of that, Masafumi. I mean, who knows what you're doing with yourself, you old devil.

As for Murph, he has lived on two islands all his life, both darlin' places. The isle of my birth is an extension of the Burren, the terrain made of limestone pavements with crisscrossing "grikes" or cracks in it. The isolated rocks are called "clints." As in Clint Eastwood and Zorba the Grike. There was a period of glaciers, as there always is, followed by the Namurian phase, resulting in what geologists call one of the finest examples of a glaciokarst landscape in the world. That is to say, more rocks. And weren't we Inishpeople proud.

Now, Manhattan can also be seen as an island of rocks—vertical and gleaming, to be sure, but basically rocks. Says here in "Why Do Men Love Islands?" that my gender consists of loners like Masafumi, that we tend toward isolation, that we all would like to be Robinson Crusoe, that we swoon for the sea, and that we're antisocial romantics. I say it's the rocks.

LET TWO PAIRS of rowers start out toward each other from opposite ends of the ocean. Let one pair embark from Inishmaan and the other from Manhattan, and let them sing shanties as they go. Let the ocean be difficult for them, tossing and menacing. Let them think of giving up and turning back. But let them not turn back. Let them row in stippled strokes through the inhospitable sea, and the shouting weather, and the elegiac crashing of the waves. After a long time, let them reach sight of each other in midocean at last, and let them wave in joy and triumph. When they pull their boats alongside each other, let them weep and embrace. Let them inquire of each other's health, and of their families' health, and of their genealogies and roots. Let them praise each other and teach each other, and offer solace. Let them sing to each other, tell tales to each other, propose commercial enterprises to each other, and the creation of parks and cities, and galleries of art. Let them sleep and dream of the sublime. Finally, let them ask of each other why they undertook this mission in the first place. Let them not know why.

ARE YOU OUT THERE? The cry of poets everywhere. Are you out there? Meaning, not merely you at this minute, but you who exist a hundred, a thousand years from now. Are you reading old Murph, Sir Thomas James Murphy, Esq. himself. DEA, PCP, SUV, KFC? Have I done anything worthy of reaching across the plains of the years to you in your dumps or palaces? I see you walking in the stubbled fields, heads down over a book. A book! Still? Is it *The Collected Works of Thomas J. Murphy* you're reading, or, if not all the works, a work or two, a phrase or clause, perhaps a single word quoted in your version of *Bartlett's*. Even a plagiarized idea will do. Or have the secret police banned any mention of my name. Something?

Show me the palms of your hands. Show me on Skype. Nothing. The leathery puckered palms of your two-fingered hands. Nothing. Have you no interest in what went before? I may not be much, but I went before. My head teems with galaxies. Someday, in the year 5014, you too will have gone before, and if you write a poem, you too will ask, Are you out there? Of course, it is possible that at this stage of erosion you know nothing, including your own desires. You may have evolved to eyeless petunias marooned at the farthest edge of Lusitania, where there is only fog and skulls, in a place so desolate, it makes Inishmaan look like Metropolis. Yet, if you do not read me, if you do not read anyone, why kiss?

Rumors of your existence have reached headquarters. Before the mass suicides that ordinarily attend such bulletins, you might send word that someone is reading someone somewhere. Even if you have to make it up. Here I gladly abandon my ego. If nothing of mine survives, so be it. But Wallace Stevens? What of Wallace Stevens? Surely Mr. Death must have tunneled his way out of the camp, enduring the critics and other fecal matter, and found his way to you, bearing a poem or two, a line or two, or a thought. He said that poetry reveals appearances and renovates experience. Something worth preserving in that. No? Health. He said poetry is health. To your health, then. *Sláinte*. Cover your nostrils and your eyes. What is that *howling*? You?

Hard to believe that all our excursions end in ice. If I

have a past, I have a future. My projections are contained in my time capsule. Within me I hold what is to come. I need not see it. Poetry should carry my future, even if the anthologies are airy, and the range of colors is reduced to gray, and there is no light in you. No light. Then read by my light, the light of me, by my flickering hope that by some means of transport, in the pebbles and the terns, shivers news of me and mine. You are my tongue. You are my poem. Are you out there?

> Where can it be found again,
> An elsewhere world . . .
>
> —Seamus Heaney, in Thomas Murphy's
> *Book of Dandy Quotations*

DO DREAMS COUNT in the places that keep public records? Where a village stores the titles connected to land and the houses, and the histories of streets, and who lies buried in what plot in the cemetery. Has anyone ever founded such a hall for dreams? The dreams of the villagers. That would be something. Yes? The Hall of Recorded Dreams. Like that vast granite Hall of Justice built on Centre Street in New York in the 1830s, called The Tombs, where, alongside the courts, they kept inmates on Death Row, who walked across a Bridge of Sighs to the gallows. The Hall of Recorded Dreams would be even bigger than The Tombs, but it would be bright and full of life. And music playing. All the pop tunes that people hear in their minds. And there would be an Annex to the Hall, for Unrecorded Dreams that people kept to themselves, like prayers. What a field trip for schoolchildren, to walk through the catacombs and the stacks, and pluck down their family's dreams, and their friends', and their own. You could read your old man's unrecorded dreams. Here's my da's. Oh, Jeez. They're all about me.

THE HOTEL ROOM is cramped, with dark green walls. It smells of tobacco and creosote. The picture of Don Quixote over the brass bed is not the usual, in that the Don is wearing gray running shorts and a blue beret instead of the knight getup, and is holding a Bic pen instead of a lance. The fireplace requires a shilling for the heat. Finding only pesos in my bathrobe pocket, I remain cold. Somewhere Dean Martin is singing "What Are You Doing the Rest of Your Life?" so clearly, I wonder if he is in the room with me. Outside on the esplanade, a smiling couple seated at a round table with a red-checkered tablecloth are toasting each other with steins of coffee. He noodles her hair. They may be posing for an ad. At an adjacent table, a wolf and a goatherd are locked in conversation about the Ebola virus. The wolf slouches. The skull of the goatherd bulges like a purple lung. They speak in the language of the forests. A beggar approaches the table of the smiling couple, carrying a rolled-up canvas that he unfurls like the phases of the moon to reveal *Las Meninas,* the original Velázquez painting. He wears the hard shoes of an Irish dancer and a tunic of gold lamé. The couple ignores the masterpiece, and the beggar sighs, moves on, and vanishes on the road into a calamity of geese. In my hotel room sits an old DuMont TV with a circular frame for the tiny screen. W. D. Snodgrass is on the set of the *Tonight Show,* behind a heavy carved-wood desk. He is editing a manuscript. Startled, he looks up, and says, Murph? Why didn't you write?

Murph? William says. Murph? Murph? I open my eyes to find my little William beside me on the bench in the park playground, tugging at my sleeve. Murph? Were you sleeping? Christ, I mutter, scared to death. I clutch him to me.

SO I CLUTCHED HER to me. But she broke my hold, and the cloak of my trance was lifted from my shoulders and I lay on the field, eyes open to the stars in shambles. Until that time, I lived in my dream state, riding the red mare bareback in midriver, the horse snorting and shaking the water off her, splashing, and stretching her great neck. When we came to the hospital, she bolted and threw me.

I inquired after Cait. Her room was a pandemonium of tubes and sponges. It smelled of resolution. Cait herself was a pandemonium of tubes and sponges, invisible under the riot, which made it difficult to hold a conversation. So I held her instead, the tubes and sponges and the girl, now small as a name, saying this and saying that. How's life? I asked her. Life? she said. Why are you weeping, Murph? Ya big sissy. Life could not be better. Life's the best. Then she slept. And after a year or two, wouldn't you know it, she flew out the hospital window in the company of a white crow, soaring high, so very high, all that was left of her was a pinpoint of light, like a point of emphasis, deep in the firmament. Since there was nothing more for me to do after that, I rested in the bed where Cait's body had been, lay down in the depression her body had made. And I tried to fill it. But, of course, I could not.

I SAW GREENBERG weep only once. Not weep, exactly. Tear up. Have I told you about this? We were lounging in the backyard of the frame house in Sunset Park we lived in before he found Barry for himself and Oona for me. We were twenty-eight, twenty-nine, with little to do during the week but work (he at law, I at teaching Catholic girls in short plaid skirts) and tell each other stories on the weekends. I was exotic to him for Inishmaan. He was exotic to me for everything—Harvard, Yale, lacrosse, the navy. One delicious summer evening, as we stretched out in our cheap chaises, he grew quiet at something I had said that reminded him of an incident with a kid named Forrest. It was at Groton, and Forrest, a rich thug from Greenwich, began to taunt Greenberg, first for being Jewish, then for being gay. He blustered into my room, and loomed over me, Greenberg said. I sat at my desk, trying not to acknowledge him, but Forrest persisted. Hey Jewboy. Hey fag. I was bigger and stronger than he was, and I knew how to box, so I kept my cool for as long as I could. Then I told him to leave the room. He tipped my chair so that I fell to the floor on my back. Without thinking, I leapt to my feet and punched him hard in the face, four or five times in rapid succession. I heard his nose break. Then I hit him in the eyes, and I heard one of the sockets crack, too. It was all over in a matter of seconds, and he stumbled from my room, screaming and wailing. We both were just fifteen. No one ever blamed me. Not the headmaster. Not even Forrest's parents, who were too familiar with their son's foul temperament. But when Forrest was out of my room, I closed the door and wept. Why? I asked him. He had turned me into a savage, Murph, he said. Just like *him*.

ONE THING we never did. We never took revenge on the bastards. When we'd won our freedom, and could have raped their women, burned their fields, hobbled their horses, and taken apart their manses stone by stone, we did not. Know why? Because Irishmen are angels? Hardly. It was because we didn't want to create a national memory of which we'd live to be ashamed. Purely a practical measure. 'Twas that simple.

I don't know that people appreciate how much of so-called civic virtue consists of purely practical measures. We had an ancient system of land distribution on Inishmaan that sounds as if it was the result of high-minded democratic thinking. It was called rundale, and, as far as I know, it's still practiced on the island. Every landowner had three fields, enclosed by rock walls. One field was good, tillable land, one was so-so, and one was good for nothing. The distribution was the same for everyone, so that no one ever felt too rich or too poor. Now you might say that such a system presaged socialism or communism or something aggressive like that. But no one ever heard of those things on Inishmaan. And neither was rundale worked out to effect justice and fair play on the island. It was just common sense. With a system like that in place, no one would ever be knocked off for his land. And no one was.

Know why I work with the homeless? Because I feel sorry for them? Because I think everyone should do things like that? Because I believe that the homeless deserve all the kindness we can give them? Yes, on all counts. Gotcha.

WHICH REMINDS ME, I haven't looked in on the folks in the shelter in a couple of weeks. So, with nothing more pressing to do, to put it mildly, I head over to the church. Reynolds and I hug and chat. I must say, it took me a while to get used to men hugging the way we do these days. On the island, if a boyo hugged you, he was passing-out drunk. I tell the minister I've seen Arthur a couple of times recently. He looks in pretty good shape, I say—I mean, for Arthur. Good shape? says Reynolds. Arthur the Bear? You haven't read about Arthur? I haven't read about anybody, I say. Poor Arthur, says Reynolds. Last Monday, in the middle of the afternoon, he climbed into a cage at the park zoo, the one vacated by Gus, the polar bear who died a couple of years ago. He bounded around on all fours and swiped his arms in the air like paws and reared up, as if on hind legs. Zoo visitors thought he was playing at first. Then they recognized the horror. Arthur had gone totally mad. The Bear became a bear. He's in Manhattan State now. You know? The mental hospital near the East River? They have him in an isolated cell. Can he receive visitors? I ask. I went yesterday, says Reynolds. It's pointless. I think, Poor Arthur. What do we know? What do we ever know?

THE OTHER DAY, the TV had a news story about a Piper Cub in Florida. The pilot radioed that he was running out of gas, and that he was going to make a forced landing on a nearby beach. As he was bringing down his plane, a little girl was walking near the edge of the water. The wing of the plane clipped the little girl and decapitated her. The pilot was unhurt. What do we ever know? If the girl had not been walking in that exact spot, if the pilot had better calculated the amount of fuel in his tank before taking off, if he'd chosen another beach, if she'd chosen another beach, and so forth. As it was, the pilot climbed out of his cockpit, looked around in gratitude for his safety, and saw the head of a little girl bobbing in the surf.

WHAT DO WE KNOW? Poets like to revel in the power of language. Words. Glorious words. But there's Gabriel in "The Dead," who also thinks that words constitute a life and a love. And there's Joyce, too, who believed in words as an artist, even as he picked apart Gabriel's narcissisms. It's nice that we believe in the power of words, but that power is nothing compared to the power of the life it aspires to represent. A Piper Cub. A little girl. Nothing. Sometimes I think writers suffer from a vanity about words, and this leads to a smugness of thought, a silly self-satisfaction and an undeserved ennobling. My da would have looked away in contempt and spat a chaw. "Brown penny, brown penny." Yes, Michael Furey was passionate. Yes, he died for love. Yes, Gretta yearned for that passion,

and Gabriel will never know it. But what is all this to a life
of real struggle? Arthur the Bear's poor life, for example.
If you ask me, Maria of "Clay" is more alive (read heroic)
than the whole lot of 'em in "The Dead," because she dares
to wake up every morning and face life in the laundry. The
daughter of a friend, another poet, died a few years ago.
Billy Collins wrote him, "Sometimes there are no words."
It was a beautiful thing to say, and also right. Sometimes
there are no words. And when we come upon those times,
we are not living in "The Dead" or writing "The Dead." We
are dwelling helplessly in life, on the sunny beach in Florida. I love being a poet. And I do the best I can to make my
writing useful (aesthetically, philosophically, practically)
for others. But not for a moment do I think that my words
are equal to life. If anything, they prove how inadequate
I am to the grand discombobulation. So maybe that's the
true power of words—to show us how puny they are in the
face of everything they attempt to say. And maybe that's
why poets write, to show the power of our powerlessness,
in a storm at sea.

TWO LETTERS, back to back:

    Dear Murph, My demi-thought of the day: Jack has
    disappeared. But does anybody disappear? I don't
    mean in the way of Amelia Earhart, Judge Crater,
    and Jimmy Hoffa. I mean every one of us. Memory

keeps us all alive, so no one ever dies and no one disappears. D. B. Cooper. Didn't you see him last week, shopping in Bergdorf's? Elvis? I'm sure that cop on the beat is Elvis. Not that I want to elevate Jack to the realm of disappeared celebrities. But whether he shows up or shows up dead, he cannot disappear. He lives in my mind, even in yours. This is immortality, isn't it? I read that Lewis Thomas said that while he did not believe in reincarnation, he had to concede the scientific proposition that nothing in nature ever disappears. So people remain, loitering in the corners of our recollections. As ever, Sarah.

Dear Murph, Still nothing from or about Jack. Is he dead, do you think? Murdered by someone he bounced in his bar? Or by his girlfriend? If she did it, depending on the circumstance, I might serve as a character witness for the defense. I don't mean that. Just a wisecrack. I don't wish Jack ill. I'm not even sure I want him back. The first couple of weeks were hard. But now it's different. You know the song "I Get Along Without You Very Well"? About someone who doesn't mean it? I mean it. I do miss the little noises. The silence gets to me. But I'm not sure I miss Jack. What was your wife like, Murph? Let me guess. Irish no-nonsense? I think she had to be that way because she married nonsense, for balance, just as you married good sense. These winter days are lovely, are they not? The wind kicks up, sways you as if you were dancing with it. You poets make a fancy fuss about the snow and rain. If I were you, I'd take up the wind. It's an under-appreciated element of nature. Do it, Murph. A poem about wind. As ever, your windbag, Sarah.

SHE HAS SOMETHING there, about silence, Sarah does. It can get on your nerves, seep into your skin, especially when you contrast it with sounds you are used to, as Sarah is doing now. But there's more to it, don't you think? There are two kinds of silence, it seems to me. One is that place where we tuck our thoughts and feelings. You can betray in silence, brood in silence, envy, pity, plot, yearn, admire, condemn, lie to yourself, lie to your conscience, forgive yourself, forgive others, all in silence. Love. You can love in silence. You usually do.

Which leads to the second kind of silence, where you find yourself from time to time, surrounded by, engulfed in—that greater silence, to which all other silences run, when you realize that we are all part of the same poem, the same vast poem that began in the first cosmic spark and will end at the last amalgamation of the stars—a limerick, a sonnet, a fucking epic to which surrender becomes a kind of understanding. It's as if sound, all sound, constituted an intrusion people invented because they could not stand the overwhelming power of that silence. We Cro-Magnons knocked off the Neanderthals because we could not bear their silence. That's Murph's theory anyway. The Neanderthals, bless 'em, had the horse sense to keep their mouths shut. Da would have approved of the Neanderthals.

Take the silence of Jesus and Mary when they were starting out. Will you? She rocking him in that stable. So quiet. Silent night, holy night. Not a bang or a whimper. Just sitting and rocking there, in the presence of absence, serene and dazzled by the mystery in which both were involved. This silence in our ears, in our blood, that roars at our imaginations. We can't take the din. We love the din.

On the island, the silence began in my little bed, then seeped out under the door of my room into the kitchen, where it flung itself from wall to wall, thence to the road outside the cottage, on which it hesitated at first, then took off like a bat out of heaven, and ran to Gallagher's field, where the men were making rope, thence to Synge's Chair, thence to the Atlantic and America, where it beat Columbus by a hair and settled in Jamestown and Plymouth and the great New York, which gave it the star treatment for a while, until it realized it had to go west and farther west, curling round Cape Horn, and eventually sailing east again, reentering my cottage and my kitchen and my sheets.

IN THE LAST FIELD on the left, just before the land slopes to the sea, lies silent Cait, beneath a murder of crows. They pace and strut. Their interest in death is purely edible, not standing on ceremony, but rather stomping noiselessly, looking at one another or at the rocks, perpetually in motion. What Thomas Gray would have made of this site I can only guess—the one-grave cemetery, not holy enough for a churchyard. Home tombing. They bury family dogs like that.

The rain's tracery on the windows distorts the picture for those inside the cottage, the scene concealed in ice crystals. Perhaps they don't look out anymore. Perhaps they have forgotten that anything resides there with the crows and rocks, the dark gray of the earth with which Cait, by now, has merged. I do not forget. Under turgid clouds in this perpetual motion city far away, I raise Cait.

DID YOU THINK I'd forgotten the brain scan? Okay. I won't offend you with the old joke about the scan showing nothing, because in fact it did indicate that my wonderful brain is ebbing a bit. Some science shit about my beta-amyloid plaques, and my neurofibrillary tangles, to say nothing of my reactive gliosis. I could have told Dr. Spector all that beforehand. She showed me the image, saying that my scan revealed hippocampal atrophy. Could have told her that, too. Christ, any hippo that has been camping out in a man's brain all these years is bound to atrophy. So what do you make of all this, doc? I ask the little cutey. Nothing yet, she says. But I can give you a blood test, something new, that can tell you if you have the e-4 gene, and are likely to develop Alzheimer's. There's nothing certain about it. You could have the e-4, and be okay. In any case, there are new experimental drugs to slow cognitive decline in high-risk patients. Would you want to take the blood test?

Why do you ask? I say. Because a lot of people would not want to know, Mr. Murphy. If the results are positive, they might get withdrawn, depressed. Withdrawn? Depressed? I say. Not I, doc. If the test shows I'm not going to get Alzheimer's, I'll dance a jig, of course. But if it shows I have that little e-4 sucker, I'll dance a jig, too, though I might forget I did it. Win, win, doc. That's what I say. If you and Máire know I'm getting Alzheimer's, you'll treat me so much better, more sympathetically. Think of the stuff I'll get away with. Poor Murph. He doesn't know what he's saying. He doesn't know what he's doing. Sings in the courtyard. Strangles Danny Perachik like a dog. By the time I'm caught, my guilt will be a moot point. Bring on the test, doc.

She regards me as if I were an experimental animal myself. Hmm, she says. The same wiseacre who was intent on subverting all these procedures a few weeks ago is now gung ho to try anything. I wonder if you're experiencing what they call a "final lucidity" that sometimes happens to people at the end of their lives. Yes. That must be it, Mr.

Murphy. A final lucidity. She studies my face. Joke, Mr. Murphy. If you're scared, I don't blame you.

Me? Scared? I say. Well, I didn't want to lie to her outright. So we make a deal, the doc and I. I shall take the blood test to learn if I'm programmed to lose my mind. Fate, do your stuff. If the test proves positive, I'll go for the experimental drugs, too. What would I have to lose? I can't wait to call Máire, to tell her that her old man has come over to her side, and is at last taking care of himself. Oh, Dad, she says. I'm so happy. When will you take the test? What test? I ask.

WHAT I MISS MOST, Oona, it's curious, I know, is the first time we met. Here's why. Because if I could have that moment back, I could savor you rather than savor me savoring you. You have no idea how lovely you looked that day, like a gesture linking intelligence, sex, and grace, all bundled in you. A look capable of understanding and forgiveness on the large scale—not forgiveness for this transgression and that, but rather for the whole race, as if you were embracing all human ecstasy and error in your smiling eyes. When Greenberg introduced us—Oona, here's Tom Murphy. He's a poet—your look had interest in it, so naturally, vain cockhead that I am, I thought about myself. Was she impressed at meeting an honest-to-God poet? Did she like what she saw? I wondered only how you were judging me.

If I could get that first meeting back, I'd cut me out of the picture and focus only on you. That's how I'd make best use of the time. I'd hear only your voice and behold only your smile and lose myself in the experience, the way Keats talks about dying into life—lose myself and dream into you, as I try to dream into life when I write. I would stop all the clocks around us, too, so that we might freeze our moment, freeze the shot the way they do in movies. The brown redness of your long hair, the firmness in your face, your shoulders, arms, would be there before me. I would lack for nothing.

There were times over the long years when I'd catch you catch the light. Standing in the park, or in the hallway. Unaware that I was watching. And then you would see me, and you would be embarrassed by my admiration and shoo me off with a wave. If I notice a similar light these days, I picture you under it. That's but one of the things that bring you back to me. A little girl on a trike looks like Máire. A piano playing somewhere in the building. A crash of dishes on the day you cracked your hip. Someone sings "Come Rain or Come Shine" or "True Love." A tapping on a pipe. I hear your two-step. All connections are welcome to me, and precious. My endometrial dancer.

But if I could have just one moment back, it would be that first meeting, which was like a word one puts in a poem, a noun probably, since nouns contain the power of things. A word you search for all your life. And who shows

up bearing that word but the great Greenberg? Figures.
The word, the one and only word, standing in front of me,
extending her hand.

UNTITLED
　　for Greenberg
　　(draft)

　　　　If at last I wandered
　　　　Past the monody of the surf
　　　　Into a place of pure beauty and kindness,
　　　　What would that look like? I ask you.
　　　　You walk ahead of me. You ought to know.
　　　　Summer grass on fire? The screaming of a beast?

　　　　I have been pursuing you
　　　　To ask about all this. And now that I am near,
　　　　You say there is nothing to report. We have
　　　　　　wandered
　　　　Into a place of pure beauty and kindness
　　　　　　together,
　　　　You say. We are unmoored, you say.
　　　　Is that not sufficient?

　　　　Truth you will not tell.
　　　　Truth is for later.

WINTER ENTOMBS US. Trees icicled. The rivers, padlocked. Our hearts, padlocked. The ball bearing of the
Earth grinds its gears toward the light at last, and the sea,
solemn sea, sheds its discipline. I am five, on the strand
tonight, looking for a sign. Even now, at this frightened
age, one feels the shadow of truth. I have lain under
the cold stars at night before Ma called me in, yearning to remember something I never experienced. I knew
who I was. Beside the white, beaten stones, I watched the
sheep huddle, and the unbroken horses and I knew who
I was.

How slick the petals of the ocean as they bloom again.
How fierce, how businesslike the tern in its hieroglyph-
ics. The Earth grinds on its axis, the strident wind goes
slack, and the stars are steady as my gaze. I would travel
now, if I could. I would walk across the ocean, past the
startled fish and dreaming whales until I reached some
shore of thought and language. Not this night, though.
On this night I am content with a ripple of warm air and
the horizon's ambiguity.

So many times like this, before. So many yet to come,
with my dull ignorance cracking open the padlocks and
straining toward the spring. I need rigor. I need geom-
etry. I need to settle into a form. My form. Me. I must
create the sensibility by which I am understood. How do
I know such things, at five? How do I know them without
knowing? The way the Earth senses the new season, I

imagine, for having known it before. When did I know it before?

AS A POET, I have to believe in God, though I have little affection for the God I believe in and he has none for me, none that he shows, anyway. Yet I must believe, or I could not write words, structure, anything. The whole process of writing a poem is mystical, to me at least, mystical and beyond my reach. Have I told you about this? I begin a poem with an image out of nowhere (where did that come from?), and at once suspect I am part of a plan, and the poem I've begun is part of a plan. The process of writing, then, is the progression toward someone else's design. And who could that someone else be but God. It's why, I think, whenever a poet arrives at the end of his poem, the moment is always unsatisfactory, a letdown. Because you think: Is this all he had in mind? But there you are, nonetheless, sweating like a pig and breathing hard, and knowing you've tried your hardest to fulfill what was decreed, preordained. And, of course, you've failed.

It's why I tend to write simple poems with rocks in them. I have throes of fanciness in me—I have to beat them down sometimes—but generally I dismiss them as fake thinking, as fiddling with knowledge or language for the silly sake of doing it. I know that dandyism does not make for real poetry. Arse poetica. This comes from my da, too. He could not stand waste—of time or behavior or language. He'd tell me, Most talk is horseshit, but not as useful. So he always spoke in a straightforward way, putting one word in a slot where a lesser man would have stuffed three. Thus every word he said was, to me, beautiful.

There is a connection between this simplicity and my feeling that a poem of mine has been written before I write it, that I am tracing the original drawing, the way children trace. And, in that same way, the tracing is different from the drawing beneath it, even if it follows the lines as carefully as the child is able. As a poet, there is always something uniquely yours in the traced work, something your own that even the original artist may not have divined. Like those copyists of the Old Masters who were compelled to leave a clue that they, mere copyists, existed too. And to reach that point in a poem, it is best to keep the language simple, like my da's, so as not to muck the thing up.

What happens, then, even though you know you have failed to follow the plan perfectly, is that you've done something worthwhile on your own, imperfectly. You have kept it simple, but it is not simple. The poem has taken you to the edge of the sea, to the point where the vast sea is revealed. And though you know you cannot re-create the sea, with all its welts and fathoms, with its treasure ships half buried in the sand on the bottom, among the kelp, and its killing fish and its killing winds and manacles, still, you have brought yourself to the brink of revelation on that shore. And the beginning of revelation is, for all intents and purposes, revelation.

You never crash if you go full tilt. It takes a kind of courage to write a poem—my ma's and da's courage, and Cait's courage, and Oona's, when she was certain she was doomed, and Sarah's courage too, when she was little and knew that she had to live all her coming days in the dark, and yet got on with it. The courage to gun it, even though you're predetermined to fail. Because between that certainty and the attempt to refute it is life, boyo—dreadful, gorgeous life.

HOW DO WE KNOW that God isn't in Hell, and Satan in Heaven, where he started out? Whose word do we have to go on? Dante? Milton? Literature is literature, my esteemed geniuses, but those poems of yours are just grand guesses. What if God simply couldn't take Lucifer's complaining and posturing and Sturming and Dranging day after day, night after night, and decided to pack his bags, get out of there, and go straight to Hell, to put as much distance as possible between himself and that irritating cocky bastard. And once that happened, let's say that Lucifer calmed down and remained in Heaven among his fellow angels, who never gave a shit about him anyway, happy that the pious asshole was out of his sight, yet sulking that he had no enemy in his weight class worthy of railing against, or usurping. And let's say that these two impressive personages have lived in both locations all along, from the start. So we have Lucifer out of place among the vanilla goody-goodies, and God sitting around with the fire and brimstone, and a bunch of cackling junior devils. Wouldn't those newly dead people assigned to one place or the other be in for the surprise of their lost lives when they got there. Good would be mixed in with evil, evil with good. And God would exist in eternal confusion. And Lucifer, too. Just like the rest of us. Thus spake Murph.

JACK LEFT SARAH a voice mail. He was safe. He was happy. He had found "the love of my life." He hoped Sarah would "understand." He apologized "for causing you so much pain." But a man "has to follow his heart." He didn't know what else to do, so he'd "just bolted." He hoped Sarah would "find it in your heart to forgive me eventually." He thanked her for "all their great years together," but he was sure she had recognized that their marriage had "gone stale." That was it, Sarah told me. After eight years, a voice mail. What a mess, Murph. He's a mess. That's one word for it, I said. Her voice went in and out. She was having trouble completing sentences. She stammered. Are you crying, Sarah? Not for him, she said. Not for our marriage. It's just sad, Murph. I thought I'd forgotten how to be sad.

ON A DARK EVENING in the early 1900s, Synge was boarding a train in the west, headed for a celebration in Dublin honoring the memory of Charles Parnell, the great nationalist leader. A wild crowd filled the station platform, many of them from Aran. Hooligans and drunks, for the most part. In the carriage compartment, a little girl from Connaught was seated next to Synge.

When the train started moving, a fight broke out among soldiers. The women who followed them were in a rage, too, cursing and swearing. Soon the women shifted moods from anger to lamentations, equally frantic. The little girl beside Synge began to cry, while a sailor in the compartment talked nonstop with what Synge described as "a touch of wit or brutality and always with a beautiful fluency." Nothing appealed to Synge more than the wild temperament of the west.

The girl began to shed her shyness and allowed Synge to point out the countryside that was coming into view in the dawn light. He described the trees to the girl, who was too small in her seat to see out the train window. He described the shadows of the trees. "Oh, it's lovely," she said. "But I can't see it." Her quiet appreciative presence contrasted notably with the strange wildness of the elders, and this mixture of moods made up the spirit of the west of Ireland to Synge—all of it moving east on a train full of people bound to pay homage to the dead Parnell. Would Sarah like Ireland?

ENTER MÁIRE, bearing plans. Apparently I need to get out more, to walk a mile a day, and focus. I need to focus. You're at sixes and sevens, she says. Thirteen, I say, and ask if this is another numbers test. She snarls. It's always worth getting Máire riled, just to see Oona again. Same rippled brow. Same scowl. I picture her scolding her clients. She does wonders with other people's money. That much I know. A guy I met at a reading told me, your daughter's a genius. I gave him a free book. My genius jabbers on. When a word of mine slides in edgewise, I ask her how she's doing. Got a new boyfriend. She says I'd like him because he reminds her of Greenberg. Gay? I ask. Not so you'd notice, she says. I'd like to put her on top of a cake.

Who's that in the picture on your desk? she asks. Dad. Daad? A wicked smile and a brightening of the eyes. Do you have a girlfriend? Nah, I say. That's just a new friend. Uh-huh, she says. Uh-huh, I say. Uh-huh, she says. Christ. Am I blushing?

Know what she does the day she tosses Fuck Hughie

out on his ear? She comes over and sits where she's sitting now, and before her mother and I can dish out the predictable bromides and consolations, she tells us, don't worry. The two of you taught me to play fair and square with the world even when the world doesn't play fair and square with me. I'll be fine. I wanted you to know that. I tried not to look over at Oona because I knew she was bawling. I couldn't see anything anyway, though eventually I made out the Kleenex. Ach Murph. You sentimental old fart. How about a drink? Don't mind if I do.

So, I'm thinking she's about to go, when she says the three dreaded words. By the way, Murph, her voice slower and more hesitant, there's something I've been meaning to tell you. By the way, she says, William and I are moving. I have a new job offer. Big and important, Murph. You'll be proud of your little girl at last. She knows I'll say, Always have been, so I say it. It's a huge investment company, she goes on. Billions, all over the world. And I'm in charge of a chunk of it. My eyes narrow. And just where in the world will you and William be going to be in charge of this chunk? I ask. London! She tries to make the word happy, but of course that's impossible. London! My outcry echoes into the misty centuries. London! As in London, England? She laughs. Is there any other kind? she says. Well, that takes the cake, I say. You sashay in here and announce not only are you moving away from your poor old father, but that you're kidnapping the best friend he has in the world in the bargain, livin' the life. Taking my grandson into the house of the enemy.

Please don't look at it that way, Dad. This is an amazing opportunity for me, and for William too. New country. New schools. And no Murph, I say. You can visit us, she says. We'll come to you. It's just a few hours away. It's a civilization away, I say. But, she says, you can see why I've been concerned about you living on your own. I wanted to make sure you were looked after before we took off. Even if you have that e-4 gene, she says, Dr. Spector's on the case. I think, Whoopie! My eyes grow narrower still. And did William know about this? I ask. She says, I just told him this morning. And what did he say? She gulps. He said, Is Murph coming with us? Whenever my heart sinks, I get belligerent. Oh missy, I get it now. London, fucking England, is just a few hours away when it means a social call, but it's a distance of light-years when you're in charge of a chunk of the world, and can't be bothered to think about your old man's mental health.

Now she looks the way she did as a little girl, when she thought she'd done something to displease me. And, as I always did then, I relent. It's her life, after all. And this all may be for the best, as I am thinking about my falling asleep when I should have been watching William— though, Christ, what will I be doing walking in Central Park without my little man beside me? I give her a hug nonetheless, and tell her it's great and that she's great and the job sounds great and that I'll be great, and that I'll swallow my pride and try to learn to speak English. And I dance her out the door before she can see my fucking eyes.

DEAR SARAH, I got me a Perkins Brailler because it's unnatural to be on the receiving end all the time, without writing back. I hope you don't mind, but you can't expect an Irishman to keep his big mouth shut too long. Bad for the lungs. He'll suffocate himself. I've been thinking a lot about Aran lately, my Inishmaan. Did I write that? *My* Inishmaan? Have you ever been to Ireland? If I drive out some of my darker memories, the way Saint Patrick is said to have driven out the snakes, the place returns to me as beautiful. Full of brave, kind, and gracious people. And lots of laughs. A red rag on a hedge. That's what it is. A flash of life and color caught in a hard place with thorns. But the thorns reveal the color of the rag as much as the rag reveals the thorns. A red rag on a hedge. I think you'd like Inishmaan. As ever, Murph.

PS. There never were any snakes in Ireland in the first place. Patrick was full of shit. Maybe my dark memories are fiction, too. You never know.

PPS. Tonight I plan to go out in the courtyard and sing

"What Are You Doing the Rest of Your Life?" I've done it before. Lovely tune. Do you know it?

PPPS. I'm giving a reading at the 92nd Street Y next Wednesday night. Want to go? With me, I mean.

YOU NEVER CRASH if you go full tilt. Sure. But one morning you look around, and you're the only driver on the road. You can say that has nothing to do with your attitude. You are Mario Andretti at any age, and you go go go whether others are there or not. And there are no more cigarette butts in the ashtrays, no more ashtrays, or big laughs and not a drop taken where once it was taken, and you thought you heard a cough but it was a dead limb cracking and falling, well then, all you have left is the books to stave off the obvious. That, and a few ripe berries.

Through the Christmas season, TCM shows a montage of the people in movies who have died during the year. Why do I weep at the sight of Greer Garson, Ronald Colman, Lana Turner, Elisha Cook Jr., Van Heflin, Butterfly McQueen, and Burgess Meredith? I knew them not. Yet they were part of my life, of all our lives. They made an impression. Burgess Meredith, not croaking and creaking in *Rocky*, but rather Burgess Meredith in *Winterset*, under the Brooklyn Bridge, young and yearning, with an old, crackling-cellophane voice way back then. But it's not just the movies we saw these people in. They went full tilt, you see. People in movies have to go full tilt, because their lives are compressed into 90 minutes or 120. And you realize that they too, the gone, surveyed the scene at some point in their lives and saw all the others gone. They left the theater alone, and hunted for a cab.

What I love about being a poet is that I see the world as a poem—a thing that lives between the lines, between the nodes, as Sarah puts it. Trouble is, those spaces increase as life increases. Mystery compounds mystery. And then one afternoon you want to say to someone, Look at this. Will you? And as you say that, you glance to your right, and Oona's gone. And you glance to your left and Greenberg has gone too. And Máire and William soon gone. Not dead, thank goodness. But gone. They become part of the space. They add to the invisible mass. Do I want to be the last man driving, only to assess the empty world as existing between the lines?

There's much to say for space, much to say for my da's gone leg, except when there's nothing to contrast it with. Burgess Meredith. Whenever they invoke *The Twilight Zone*'s greatest hits, they trot out old Burgess, wandering the wasteland city in search of peace and quiet and something to read. When he crushes his eyeglasses underfoot by mistake, that's supposed to be the tragedy of the tale. But the tragedy comes before that, when he wanders around and no one is there. It wasn't a small tragedy—poor Burgess not being able to go into seclusion with his beloved books. It was the greater tragedy. He could not see other readers. Maybe I ought to join AARP after all, and enjoy the many benefits of membership.

My hands loosen their grip on the wheel, and I shoot forward into the empty supermarket, and out again into the empty stadium, and out again. I drive to Bethlehem, Paris, Akron. Not a soul anywhere. I drive to Tinian, whence the *Enola Gay* took off for sleeping Hiroshima. I drive the runway, now weeds and midges, built extra-long for the weight of the bomber. Nothing there. Nothing in the hospitals in Galway. Nothing in the swimming pools in Mamaroneck, or in the Belnord courtyards, either one. Nothing in the New York Public Library, not even Burgess Meredith. I blast through the stacks, going a hundred, maybe two. Look. No hands. Go Oona. Go Greenberg. Go William. Go Máire. From here you look like berries.

In memoriam, everyone. Much love.

AFTER THE READING, we go to a bar on Third Avenue, with photographs of dogs covering the walls. I describe some of the dogs to her. She asks how they are dressed. We chat about this and that, but not about Jack. I'm relieved. I think she is, too. She says she liked the reading, but thought the Q&A afterward was a waste of time. Always is, I tell her. A novelist friend of mine deliberately times his readings to end within ten seconds of the hour allotted, so

as to eliminate room for the Q&A. Even so, I went to one of
his readings where a guy got his question in within those
ten seconds. He asked my friend how to get an agent. Some
of the greatest Q&A moments occur at the 92nd Street Y, I
tell her, because Jews are so crazy. They're Irishmen, I'm
certain of it. Ireland, a lost tribe of Israel. Same gloom,
same jokes, same fight in 'em. Same fixation on one point
of view. I tell her of the time I finished a reading of poems
at the Y that I, for one, thought moving and heartbreaking.
A bearded guy in the front row raises his hand, and says, I
saw you on TV. Not knowing how to answer that question,
I scanned the room in search of another. From the back,
a woman calls out, I saw you on TV, too. Then the first guy
pipes up again. On TV, he says. I saw you on TV.

Crazy kikes, I say. Crazy micks. I love those words, says
Sarah. I know you're not supposed to say them. But they
have such life. Coons. Wops. Yes, I say. And most are one
syllable, giving them a special kick. Gook. Hebe. Slope.
Jap. Chink. We go on like that, trying to come up with all
the delicious slurs and verbal no-no's forbidden in polite
company, all one syllable. Cunt. Fuck. Cock. Tits. Which
reminds me, she says. Why are you men so taken with
our tits? It goes back to our babyhood, I tell her. We long
to suckle. Bullshit, she says. It's because you're such an
uninteresting gender. Even blind as a bat, I can tell when a
man is staring at my tits. Am I staring at them now? I ask.
(I am.) Of course you are, she says. If I wanted to make

all men happy, I'd wallpaper their houses with pictures of tits, the way these walls have dogs. Bitch, I say. Dick, she says.

DEAR MURPH, I've been involving you in a plan about light this morning. Most blind people are able to make out light from dark. I cannot. The condition is called NLP, no light perception. Been this way from birth, which means that all I know of light comes from what others tell me, or what I read. You could say, I've been in the dark about light. This may exaggerate the importance of light in my mind. You know? The thing one cannot attain? Not that I have a quarrel with darkness. Sometimes I'm bored with it, the way anyone might be bored with one's hometown, from which he may never travel. But the mere suspicion of light, the mention of it, is enthralling to me. I picture sailors in a black storm at sea, suddenly spotting the beam from a lighthouse. Or the proverbial tunnel with the light at the end of it. I've listened to movies in which a blind person has his sight restored by an operation. The bandages are removed, and oh my! Someday, Mr. Poet, I'd like you to tell me what light is like, so that at last I might see it in my darkness. Think you could do that? As ever, Sarah.

RIDING FAST in the darkness, past a rotted bole, I came
to a rock wall. It stood no higher than three feet, an easy
jump for me and the horse. We had taken jumps higher
than that lots of times, higher and deeper, without hesita-
tion. But on that tarnished-silver afternoon, with the sun
in hiding and the sky turned black, the horse refused. At
the approach, instead of gearing up the way horses do, it
veered off to the side of the wall, and we swung away.

Which one of us refused to take that jump, do you
think? In his book, Professor Dodds uses this very situ-
ation as an example of the unconscious at work. But long
before I read Dodds, I lived the riddle. Who faltered? The
horse or the rider? If I say it was I who refused to take
the jump, the explanation is rational. At that particular
moment on that particular afternoon on the island of
Inishmaan, I made a conscious judgment that whatever
past experience may have told me to the contrary, we were
not going to clear that wall.

But if it was the horse that decided to veer to the side,
then something wholly irrational may have been at work in
that field. The animal had become the instrument of my
subconscious, and for no discernible reason—no premoni-
tion of danger, nothing like that—it decided to go its own
way. The horse had refused to take the wall not out of fear,
but in rebellion to something hidden from us both, and
never to be understood by either of us. From such impulses
madmen murder, poets write, and old fools fall in love.

GO AHEAD, he said. Plant one on me. Standing next to me
at the bar in At Swim-Two-Birds is Jack, out of nowhere,
with his hat in his hand, and his face a sea of gloom. Do it,
Murph. I deserve it. Give me a shot to the kisser. And he
juts out his big jaw. What do you want, Jack? I turn away.
To apologize, he says. It's not me you need to apologize to,
boyo. I know, I know, he says. I tried to tell her how sorry
I am in a voice mail, but . . . Sarah quoted it to me, I tell
him. It could not have been more pathetic. Ya see? he
says. Ya see? Pathetic. I don't even know when I'm being
pathetic. But it's always the same with Sarah, Murph. I
can't tell her about important things, the things I feel,
'cause I don't know how to relate to her. She's better than
I am. Smarter, educated. No matter what, I screw up. He
sits beside me, uninvited. Why don't you have me apologize for you? I ask. That way she'll be sure to know it's
bullshit. How's your colon cancer, by the way, Jack? Acting
up, is it? Look, he says. I know I did the wrong thing. But I
wasn't really lying to you. I've never had the nerve to talk
to Sarah. And Christ, I couldn't tell her about Peggy Ann.
I mutter, Peggy Ann. So I came up with this harebrained
scheme involving you. All wrong, I do know that. But the
reason I did it, Murph, that was the truth. I don't have the
words.

   Boyo, you may have made a career spouting this kind
of horseshit, I tell him. But don't expect me to go along,
and clap you on the back. Let me be clear, Jack. I don't

accept your apology. Not because you hoodwinked me. I can handle myself. But you hurt a wonderful woman, who has it hard enough without being saddled with a lying, cheating fuck-off who thinks he can talk his way out of any jam he makes. Jesus, Jack. Look at yourself. You say you don't have the words. Fuck, man. Words is all you have. What you lack is a sense of basic decency. He turns away.

Give me a break, Murph? A little slack? There are two sides to every story, you know. I roll my eyes. It's no picnic living with Sarah, he says. I mean, she's wonderful, like you say. But she's hard, too. There's no give to her. And what sort of give are you looking for, Jack? Permission to butt-fuck every Peggy Ann who winks and hikes up her skirt? Now, that's not fair, Murph, he says. You don't know Peggy Ann. No, boyo. But I know Sarah, a little at least. And what I know is that all she asks of life is a straight shooter. She cannot see what's going on around her. She's vulnerable to every drunk driver, every careless kid on roller skates or a bike, every pickpocket and exuberant joker who gesticulates as he babbles along the street and bumps into her and says, Hey lady, why don't you look where you're going! That is what the world is like for Sarah, Jack, which you, more than anyone, ought to know. So, it isn't too much to ask of the man who's married to her, who has promised her his love and protection, to treat her as if she exists.

Jesus, Murph. You sound as if you know her better than I do. I signal Jimmy for another. Let me ask you something, Jack. What sort of woman did you think you were getting in Sarah, when you married her eight years ago? You must have recognized how smart she is, how plain damn good she is. How kind, he says, I saw how kind she was, is. I guess I needed kindness. You don't know anything about me, Murph. Actually, Sarah knows very little herself, because I'm ashamed. Ashamed of my folks who were blackout drunks, and the Quonset hut we lived in near the Navy Yard. And the screaming all the time. And the banging on the walls. And the filth that never washed off. And Mr. Porty next door, with the greasy hands, who gave me a dollar for every blow job. The only thing I could do well as a kid was swim. In the summers I escaped to Riis Park, and when I got big enough they trained me as a lifeguard. That's how I got out of the Quonset hut. I swam out. The lifeguard board located me in East Hampton. I had enough dough for a room of my own over Starbucks, where I could smell through the floorboards the coffee I couldn't afford. But at least I was out. And then, early one morning, there was Sarah, walking down the beach like a visiting angel. And I knew soon as I saw her, soon as she knocked me on my ass, that if I could be with a girl like that, I might be saved. And what about Sarah? I say. What did you think you were going to give to your angel? What were

you going to do for *her*? He shrugs and looks down at the
floor.

Oh Christ. What am I here? The Grand Inquisitor? I
could grill this dumb slob from here to Sunday, and nothing would come of it. Why am I bullying this jackass?
I should know by now, people are not to be explained or
reformed. We are what we are, what we'll always be. I never
saw a change worth warm spit in anyone past the age of
three. And the truth is, Jack isn't a bad guy. He's a battered
guy, who never received love. And I'm telling you, if you
don't receive love, if you've never received love as a child,
you're a goner. Half the kids I grew up with on Inishmaan
were Jack—not necessarily brutalized like Jack, but treated
as surplus furniture, as junk, just as their ma and da had
been treated before them. In their case, it wasn't parents
who didn't love them. It was life itself.

A writer I know was working on a memoir that, he
told me, surprised him the deeper he got into it. He had
always resented the killing coldness of his parents. For
all his life, he'd hated them. They should not have had
children, he said. But you know, Murph? he told me
at this very bar. The more I wrote about my folks, this
sin and that, I realized that all they were is people, just
people. Flawed, sure. Destructive, unconsciously cruel.
All that. But in the end, just people. That was Jack—
flawed, destructive, unconsciously cruel, yet human. As
a poet, I am supposed to understand such things. As a

man, it's more difficult. In the silence between us I find
myself resisting the impulse to give Jack a comforting
pat on the shoulder.

But I resist it anyway, and spin the big guy around
where he sits, and give him a knuckle sandwich, square in
his right eye. He rocks back, shocked. Then he laughs. So,
you forgive me, Murph?

SHE HAS ME THINKING about blindness. I never gave it
much thought before. There was a Portuguese novel I read
a long time ago, called just that, *Blindness*—about a mass
epidemic in an unnamed city. Everyone but a doctor's
wife is stricken, and she, because she has retained her
sight, is mistrusted and scorned by the blinded citizens.
One character stands out: a beautiful girl struck down
during casual sex in a hotel room. Tough and icy at first,
she is humanized by her blindness, and she takes care of
an orphan boy. When she no longer is able to see, she
finds that she can dream reality, and recognize the beautiful without seeing it. Perhaps that's why I can remember her.

Tiresias, Polyphemus, Jesus healing the blind. Milton, of course, and Homer, and Blind Lemon Jefferson
and Ray Charles and George Shearing. Others. Once
you're on the subject, the names, real and fictional,
roll out. Velázquez painted a blind woman with Sarah's

Madonna-like serenity, her eyes cast down in the portrait. H. G. Wells had a story called "The Country of the Blind." A sighted man finds himself trapped in a land where no one else can see. He endures prejudice turned on its head.

Sarah's blindness affects the way I think about her. It lends her a kind of magnetism. I am drawn to her darkness, as if I am able to join her there in the permanently dark room of her mind. Yet her mind is not dark in the sorrowful or funereal sense. It is more like a photographer's darkroom, in which it takes time for a picture to develop. She is willing to wait. I am, as well. She was born blind, and all she knows of the light comes from what she is told or what she reads. I find her darkness enlightening. My eyesight is improved by it.

One blind old woman I knew on Inishmaan. She scared the shit out of me, perched in a wicker chair before her cottage, all day, every day, even in the rain. She was not frightening because of anything she did or said, but simply because she embodied aloneness. One felt alone enough on the island, without an extra kick in the pants, like blindness or deafness, or being crippled like my uncomplaining da. Sarah feels alone, too, so she says. But I think she is using the word only technically. She appears so self-contained, one feels she needs nothing she does not seek. So she seeks me. That's interesting, because I seek her. Dancing in the dark?

SHE HAS ME thinking about sight, too, and foresight. During a phone chat the other day, out of the blue she asks how I intend to spend the rest of my life. I think about little else, I tell her. People do tend to go on these days, she says. Ten more years for you, Murph? Twenty? Any suggestions? I ask her. I'll think about it, she says. What do you see in my future, Madam Sarah? What do your tarot cards tell you? She puts on a sort-of-Hungarian accent. Your future, Meester Murphy? Your future? Better I see your past.

You've helped me see, you know, Murph. How so? I ask. Your poems see quite well. You make the reader see. But you never have seen the things I describe in my poems, I tell her. How do you know I'm right? I want you to be wrong, she says, and you never fail me. You imagine things your way, not as they are, which allows me to imagine them based on your imaginings. You make me see best, she says, when you apply your imagination to things that are real, things I know the shape of already. When you write about them, I see them your way. You have a poem about a chameleon warming itself in the tropical sun. I've never seen a chameleon, so all I know is that it camouflages itself by adopting the colors of its surroundings. What I did not know—and thanks to you I now do—is that a chameleon takes R & R.

I ask her, Do you suppose I can imagine what I'll be doing the rest of my life? For that to happen, Meester Mur-

phy, she says, you may need to imagine what you already
know.

ARTHUR ZEROES IN on me through the thick Plexiglas window in his cell door. His eyes burn deep in his fur. I do not
know what to do. I wave meekly, hoping he'll recognize me.
Arthur! His dark lips do not move. Nothing on him moves.
His doctor tells me that he has made not a sound since they
brought him in. Silent in his cell, he eats dishes of berries. Sometimes he paces, says the doctor. Mainly he stares,
watches. The hospital staff is waiting for a change in behavior, in effect waiting for Arthur to become human again.

Dark, dark. His eyes blaze blackness, like black gem-
stones in a velvet box. Do you want to kill me, Arthur?
Do you want to kill us all? There are no bears in Ireland.
They vanished in the tenth century, after the Vikings
killed them off for the pelts. I stand at the Plexiglas window for maybe twenty minutes. I do not budge. Neither
does Arthur. He doesn't flinch, doesn't blink. What do we
know? What do we ever know? Bear paws at his side. Bear
claws showing. He has scratched himself. Bear blood.

TO IMAGINE WHAT YOU already know. Solitary on the bay
side of the island, on the flats leading to the water, were
the remains of a cottage consisting of three stone walls.

One was the back of the house. Two stood at each end, where the thatched roof once had lain between them. How old the place was—a hundred years, six hundred—no one seemed to know. Do you remember who lived there? I asked my da. It stood just as it is now, when I was a boy, he said. The upper portions of the side walls looked like bookends, with no books in between. They supported only themselves. A road curved off to the right of the house, and the bay lay under clouds beyond.

Throughout my childhood, I kept waiting for the house to fall into ruin, but it did not. No one tore it down, no one rebuilt it. It belonged to no one, just standing where it always had stood, a monument to what Synge, referring to the old empty British manor houses, called the "splendid desolation of decay." Was it incomplete? I wondered, since it had been complete at one time. I felt that you called something incomplete only if you thought it was heading, or hoping, for completeness. The house was complete in its incompleteness.

Sometimes I'd take it in from a great distance, viewing the house as part of the whole Inishmaan landscape. Then it looked small to me, incidental. Sometimes, I'd stand inside the three walls, among the grasses and the weeds. Then the house seemed to constitute the world. Once I stood within the walls during a rainstorm, trying to hear what the family to whom the house had belonged and to which it belonged in turn, would have been speaking of, as the rain beat down on the thatch all those years ago. There's a leak on the east side of the roof, said the ma. The pa said, I'll see to it in the morning.

CHRIST WAS PREACHING up a storm on St. Nicholas Avenue, when I happened by. Kids paused their game of stoop ball to laugh at him and his sermon on greed and luxury. Just you wait, he told the kids, beseeching heaven for their sins. And in a New York minute, sure enough. A storm.

Do they who live here feel the strangeness that I feel? There is no sign of it. Inishmaan, Manhattan, the same. The people live where they live, and I as well, with them. Yet to me, a solitary fisherman, the bitter rains, the plumage of the ladies, the mad laughter of birds (etc., et al.), exist in a luminous incompleteness, like that three-walled cottage, as if I, and I alone, their distant, present cousin, had been created to perceive the whole. The glowing restaurant, the smoke-glass reservoir, the doorman in his epaulets, the family's promiscuous maid, Arthur the Bear—who lives where I live? Hello, stranger. I am greeted by the owner of a bookstore I haven't visited for years. Hello, stranger. She has no idea.

And the people in my building. I'm sorry to learn they complain about me and have no affection for me, 'cause I have tons of affection for them. Botsford of the blue Vespa. The Lewises. The DeBoks, natural aristocrats, whom I see every Christmas at the local soup kitchen dishing out grub. We just nod. Says everything, a nod. Mr. Jones, a widower like me, but more dignified. Who couldn't be? And Dr. Berman, the only Belnord resident crustier than I am, who grumbles past me in the hallways like a cement mixer. I speak his language. I grumble back. And relentless Mrs. Ginnilli, who keeps trying to collar me for her book club meetings, so that I'll talk poetry with the ladies. We need your brains, Mr. Murphy, says the sweet thing. Oh, I'm sorry, Mrs. Ginnilli, I tell her. I'm having my brains removed next week. All of them adorable, admirable, and to me, magical.

Time was, I am told, there was more magic in the world than world. And the red eyes of daisies and the men who spoke reindeer were as common as rocks. Whenever you wanted something, anything, you needed to do nothing but dream. Say you wanted the morning light to be condensed into a hunting bow, or to spend Easter vacation on the far side of a mirror. You had only to say so. And presto. Magic. Bring back the dead for a dance at Roseland? For one last spin around the floor? Not a problem.

DEAR MURPH, I wanted to tell you how I drowned my brother David. I was eight. He was two. We were with our parents on the beach in East Hampton, on a rainy Sunday. No one else was there, as far as I could tell. My folks never left David and me alone for more than a few minutes, and they would tie a little rope around his waist and around my wrist, so that I would feel it if he tugged. That afternoon, I had brought a braille copy of *Little Women* to the beach and I was lost in it, so I did not notice when there was no tension in the rope. Where's David? My mother fairly screamed from up the beach. David? David! We all cried. I felt the rope that had been around his waist, slack in my hands. There was a lot of screaming of David's name, both from my parents and from others elsewhere who had heard the screaming. I just sat where I had been, *Little Women* in my lap. In a few minutes I heard police and ambulance sirens. I remained sitting. My father cried, Oh God! Oh God! My mother was hysterical. I did not move. My face felt paralyzed. There! There! A man's voice. And people running in shoes on the sand. Someone said, Again. Someone else said, Keep trying. A great silence followed, and I continued to sit and listen. Finally, I heard a terrible weeping from my parents, and their footsteps as they approached my blanket. They said not a word to me till we were home.

DEAR SARAH, I wanted to tell you how I drowned my best friend Cait. We were eighteen, and had

been on-and-off lovers, but mainly friends all
our lives. In a place as small as Inishmaan, a good
friend is a treasure, and Cait was that to me. She
had the heart of a lion. Her death too, like your
brother's, occurred on a beach. We were there one
spring evening, the two of us, looking out toward
Galway Bay and the mainland. Cait brought a jug of
poteen, our Irish homemade hooch, and we were
getting pretty smashed. I was half dozing, when
Cait thought it a good idea to take off her clothes
and swim out to a rock island sticking up out of the
bay. She was always doing daring stuff like that, and
I thought little of it. I should have swum out with
her. I knew she was drunk. And then I saw her slip
off the rock and go under. When she didn't surface,
I went after her, swimming around the rock, and
calling her name the way your folks called David's.
Funny about that. We call out the names, though we
know it's no use, as if the sound of the name itself
were a lifesaving measure. But I did find her, and
brought her, still alive, to the shore. Her eyes swam
in her head, and her limbs were limp. By the time
we got her to the hospital in Galway, she was as good
as dead, the doctors said, brain dead. When I'd
carried her from the water, she felt light as a sheet
of paper.

I LIKE THIS GIRL, Oona. I'm telling you now in case any-thing develops between us, and I don't want you saying, Isn't this a fine how-do-you-do! The truth is, you would not be surprised that I like her, at least not any more sur-prised than I am. Love comes to old Murph one last time? I don't know. It may not be love yet. But as the song says, it'll do until the real thing comes along. It's just that I feel a strength in her, akin to yours, and a basic goodness, akin to yours, and a horse sense akin to yours, too. She isn't you, old girl. No one could be. But she has something that gets under my skin, in a peace-giving way, as if I knew her a long time ago.

There have been but three women in my life, that is, if Sarah qualifies as the third. One I found and lost on Inishmaan. One to whom I gladly gave my heart and vows. You know that one. And now this girl, who steps in so quietly, you'd hardly know she's there. Oh, noth-ing will come of it, most likely. There are more years that separate our ages than years she's been alive. And she's got a husband, to boot. God knows where. But still. And I really don't know if I have any love left in me, after you.

Her being blind? You might worry about that, since I'm having a little trouble taking care of one person, who at least can see what he's messing up. The odd thing is, she makes me quite comfortable with her blindness. She gets around well on her own, but that's not what I mean. Most of the time, I do not notice that she's blind. I guess age does that to you, makes you focus on what counts. And she seems comfortable not being able to see me. I try to tell her of the glory that she's missing. She fires back that my mind is so dazzling, she does not know if she could survive the blaze of my physical beauty. You can see what I like in her. It's you.

What she sees in me, I have no idea. Apart from my manly manliness, brains, and rugged good looks, I mean. Frankly, I don't really know if she sees anything in me at all. But she sees, this blind girl, Oona. She sees.

Of course, if Sarah and I do get together, I'd have to divorce you, since I still feel married to you. But divorce it must be, old girl. Sorry about that. Alert the Church and the Holy Father. Oh, is that so? you say. And divorce on what grounds? you say. The oldest, I say. Infidelity. With Heaney. And don't deny it. Heaney bought the farm less than a year ago. And I know you, Oona. You always liked him better than me, and now you have your chance. I'll divorce you for playing around with Seamus, shacking up in heaven. And you'll both live in disgrace among the angels. Just like Adam and Eve. How do you like that apple—my dearest, darlin' love?

I WHISPERED, "I am too young,"
And then, "I am old enough";
Wherefore I threw a penny

To find out if I might love,
"Go and love, go and love, young man,
If the lady be young and fair."
Ah penny, brown penny, brown penny,
I am looped in the loops of her hair.

O love is the crooked thing,
There is nobody wise enough
To find out all that is in it,
For he would be thinking of love
Till the stars had run away
And the shadows eaten the moon.
Ah penny, brown penny, brown penny,
One cannot begin it too soon.

DEAR MURPH. It occurs to me that you may be wondering why a glamorous exotic beauty such as myself would be wasting her glamorous exotic time with a possibly demented, hoary fellow such as yourself. So here goes.

They'll tell you love is blind, but not for the blind. We need to know what we're doing. And if ever we do behave as though love is blind, or should be, we wind up with our geese cooked, as I did with Jack. I'm not angry with Jack. Pissed off about there being another woman, of course, but that's more human reflex than anything heartfelt. I'm sorry for Jack. I've always been sorry for him. He has a knack for making people feel sorry for him, which is how he gulled you with his cock-and-bull story about dying. There's a sweetness and basic goodness about Jack, but his true, virtuoso gift is making people feel sorry for him. And I wonder now if I originally fell in love with him because he was in worse shape than I was, and I could take care of him, and feel less like an object of pity myself. We may have shared an eight-year marriage consisting of the blind leading the blind. Who knows.

No one feels sorry for you, Murph. You won't permit it. And that's one of the things that draws me to you. You work at one of the most selfish jobs there is—a writer. Yet your view of everything goes outward. If I employed a guide dog, it would be you (though I'd need a steel muzzle). And though you sometimes appear lost, you really aren't. You use the feeling of being lost to discover someplace better. It's where your poems come from, I'm sure of it, and where I discovered you long before we met. Your poems are unalloyed generosity. They reach for the reader's lost soul, and say, Let's lose ourselves together, and see what place we're in.

And this, too, about your poems: you never end a thought on one line without beginning another thought on the same line. Is that because you don't think anything ends? You fear death but do not believe in it, sort of the opposite of how you feel about God. Right? Nothing ends. So you're old, but you have no age. I have no idea what sex would be like with you, if you don't mind my raising the subject.

But I'll tell you this: if ever you and I do wind up between the sheets, I'll bet you it will go on and on and on, like one of your lines. And wouldn't that be fun for me, for a change.

When you're blind, you learn everything from something else. I know the location of my front door when my knuckles brush the top of a ladder-back chair in the kitchen. When I feel bread crumbs underfoot, or coffee grounds, I know it's time to sweep the floor. The dry leaves in a flowerpot tell me to water the flowers. You may think, how limited her life. In fact, it's an arrangement of endless expansions. Every element betrays its position by relating to another element, and you know the world by these implications.

So it is that I know the world through your touch. You take my hand when we walk, and you think you're protecting me. I appreciate the gesture, but the pleasure's all mine. I love touching you, and you touching me, however grazingly. I love brushing against your shoulder, accidentally or not. (You think I can't see where I'm going.) I love it when we sit side by side in a tight place, and our knees touch, bone to bone. I love to grasp your elbow, or laugh so hard that my head collides with your chest. I love the feel of your flat palm on the small of my back when you steer me from behind. If you had to reduce all the reasons for my attraction to you, it would be this nonreason. Pure unreasoned touch. So this is what I think you wanted to know, dear Murph. You are my braille.

UNDER MY FRONT DOOR slithers a letter from my landlord offering me $500,000 to give up my apartment.
Since $500,000 is more money than I make most weeks
from my poetry, I give the letter my rapt attention. After
some de rigueur niceties about how honored the Belnord
has been to have me as a tenant for the past forty years,
the letter goes on to cite my "erratic behavior" in recent
months, of which my landlord has been apprised by the
filthy, greasy, creepy crawly Daniel A. Perachik. Would
I not be happier and safer, posits my landlord, in an
assisted living facility, where people could look after me.
Teary am I that he and Perachik are so concerned about
my welfare. His proposition is worth considering for a
second and a half. If I took the money and ran, would I
be the superstar of my nursing home, king of the living
assisted, with half a million simoleons to toss around?
Think of how many kazoos I could buy. Fuck 'em. We Irish
are used to evictions.

Simoleons, yes. Never been much interested in
money, but the terms for it are grand. Simoleons. A
conjoining of *Simon,* British slang for "sixpence," and
Napoleon, French slang for "Napoleon." Moola, smack-
ers, loot, long green, a five-spot, a fin, a tenner, a grand,
lucre, dough, dead presidents, cabbage, Benjamins,
bones, folding stuff, large, sawbucks, a wad. I've spent a
lifetime shooting wads. Poets do that. We cannot bring
ourselves to care about the stuff. When Auden had a

place on Second Avenue, he was so poor he was starving to death. One day, Christopher Isherwood paid him a visit and discovered a check for $10,000 in a letter from Auden's publisher, buried under a pile of papers, that the poor man had neglected to open.

The main reason I'm so bad with money is genetic, because I'm Irish. Sure, there are a few rich Irish, like the Kennedys. My own Máire makes other people rich. But in general the chips don't suit us. The whole idea of money goes with high-hatting and putting on airs. We can be loaded, all right, just not that way. And whenever one of us has money to burn, he usually does it. Besides, poverty serves our literature. In Liam O'Flaherty's "The Informer" (speaking of Perachik), no sooner does Gypo Nolan get ahold of his twenty pounds of flesh for turning in Frankie McPhillip than he blows the reward money on booze, talks too much, is found out, and shot. There isn't a single Irish play, not Synge's or O'Casey's or Behan's, where the central problem could not be solved by eight or nine pounds. I toss the landlord's letter.

Then let the sleet and the mist and the darkness
    descend.
We'll wing our cries above them till the end.
                        —John Ennis, in Thomas Murphy's
                                    Book of Dandy Quotations

IF NOW YOU'RE EXPECTING me to paint the scene at JFK when Máire, William, and I are saying our good-byes, and bawling like bleating sheep, with William's little arms locked around my neck and Máire choked with sobs, and I a wreck-and-a-half, knees buckling, barely able to stand—well, you can whistle for it. I'm not going through that again. What I will tell you is that once they were safely off, I headed straight to an airport saloon, downed nine fingers of Jameson (three glasses, three fingers each), and dumped myself into a cab. And I will also tell you that, reeling into the Belnord courtyard, I decided that this would be the night for Botsford's Vespa. So I snatched the key off the hook in the office and started up the blue beauty. At this point, I could also tell you that I jumped aboard like a cowboy bandit, and gave the engine a few revs, and took the darlin' blue-eyed devil for the ride of its mechanical life, shooting round and round the courtyard at sixty. I could tell you that. But what really happened was that I tripped on the kickstand, and the Vespa toppled over on my right foot. And everyone in the building heard the banging, and stuck their heads out their windows like gargoyles. And Botsford ran downstairs, and good guy that he is, was more worried about me than the Vespa, and half carried me to my apartment, where I hit the bed, fell into a drunken sleep in my clothes, and dreamed that I was visited by Marilyn Monroe, Zero Mostel, and Isaac Bashevis Singer, the two men in drag like Jack Lemmon and Tony Curtis. Then we all sang "Runnin' Wild," with Isaac on sax, Zero on bass, and Marilyn on the uke. How about that?

HOW TO LIVE OLD
by Thomas J. Murphy, PC, DDS, CPA, AARP

Being old and alone is not all it's cracked up to be. Yet the last stages of living can offer great fun and many rewards if one pays heed to a few basic tenets. The following rules of conduct are intended for those who have just crossed the border of their seventies, and anticipate living on into their nineties. What should I do to make the best possible use of these added years? How best to spend my time? I'm glad you asked.

1. Cultivate your most irritating qualities. This rule may seem counterintuitive, because you have bought into the idea that old people should be sweet and wise. Well, first of all, you are not going to get any wiser in old age than you were in young age. In fact, you are likely to become a great deal stupider, and even on those rare occasions where you luck into a wise solution to someone's problem or to one of your own, by the time you are prepared to implement it, you will have forgotten it. As for sweet, why should you strain for that? It goes against all normal human inclinations. And if you walk around with a marzipan smile on your puss all the time, you will be taken

for an idiot. Everyone who is not sweet (the world's great majority) will take advantage of you. No. What you must do is to discover the most annoying qualities you displayed before you turned seventy, and triple their intensity. If you were cheap, behave so parsimoniously that your former self will seem profligate in comparison. If occasionally you were irritable, become a full-blown crank. And don't let up on any one of these tendencies. What you want is for all those around you to make your excuses for you by shrugging and sighing, ah well, he's old.

2. Ever a dull moment. Excitement is an overrated reaction to things, usually events we anticipate, such as seeing a new promising movie, or meeting a new promising friend. Inevitably all such promises, when realized, turn out to be disasters, so why not cut them off at the pass? Lower your expectations, not just a little. Lower your expectations to the subbasement. By your seventies, life has taught you that nothing is as predictable as disappointment, so listen to your broken heart. To be sure, you will not get much pleasure out of this exercise, but it passes the time, and you can always congratulate yourself on how wise the years have made you, though they haven't (see Rule #1).

3. Develop a good false stare. Old people spend much of the time staring, anyway, so no one will know when you're faking it. But your stare need not be as vacant as it appears. An old man's stare is useful for girl-watching, for instance,

without giving offense. To anyone observing you, including the object of your attention herself, it will seem that you are hypnotized, or dead, and she might even give you a sympathetic if condescending smile. I enjoy staring at the trees in Central Park. I appear to be engaging in the old brainless pastime, when in fact, I'm counting the number of greens in a grove. Sarah says she stares all the time. People think she's merely being blind, but for her it's a mode of contemplation. Naturally, the best thing about a good stare is that it keeps people from talking to you. Any activity that keeps people from talking to you is a good activity.

3a. And don't worry about being impolite. Politeness is for occasions where nothing is at stake. You never heard anyone say, Pardon me for ruining your life.

4. Watch your step, literally. After the age of seventy, you should regard your body as scrupulously as a garage attendant inspecting your car for dents. I walk up and down stairs (down is worse), as if I were stepping from stone to stone in a mile-wide Irish creek. I am as graceful as a tank. So hesitant and awkward am I descending a staircase, I have had frail schoolchildren come up to me to ask if I'm all right. Of course I'm all right, I bark. Remember when your bones were not twigs? Remember when you didn't think about your bones? Remember when you had muscles on some of them? Remember when you didn't devote every hour of every day to exquisite self-inspection? Aw, fuck it.

5. Do not attempt to make amends with past enemies. This is a common inspiration in old age, to be dismissed from the mind as soon as it enters. Oh, you'll feel cleansed and noble when you write old McMinus, and tell him, after all the long years, let bygones be bygones. But once McMinus writes back or phones, or worse, meets you for a drink, you'll remember at once why you hated the bastard in the first place. And now you'll hate yourself. Nothing is so satisfying as a well-placed bitterness. Enjoy. In a similar vein, suppress urges to visit old friends. They're fine as they are, and things can only get worse. Ditto for class reunions. These lurches lead nowhere. Relax.

5a. And if you have no enemies? Where's your sense of judgment, man?!

6. If you find yourself saying, I've wasted my life, you will. Don't say it, even if you can prove it. It's my experience that only men whine about such stuff. Women, smarter, just get on with it. Juno v. Paycock. In general don't despair, and if you must, don't force your despair on others. It's unfair to add your despair to theirs.

7. Save the world. Age affords an excellent opportunity to save the world. But you're running out of time. Know what gets Murph? He's lived seventy-plus years without having rid the world of barbarians, tyrants, traitors, cowards, bullies, murderers, liars, thieves, crooks, backbiters, and grinning accommodators. Also, he has not cured the world's diseases, from sniffles to the Ebola virus to endo-

metrial cancer. He has not prevented droughts, floods, tsu-
namis, tornados, cyclones, and earthquakes. He has not
eradicated poverty, famine, waste, ignorance, or bigotry.
He has not stopped the glaciers from melting or the trees
from falling. He has not put an end to injustice, or even
to casual cruelty. Neither has he established freedom and
goodwill everywhere. He has not seen to it that everyone
leads a useful and productive life, and exhibits only tender-
ness and generosity toward one another. He has not unified
the races, or equalized the genders, or protected and educated the children. Nothing he has done, not a single line of
a single poem, has resulted in a complete global reformation. In all his seventy-plus years, nothing. Disgraceful.

RABBI BEN MURPHY

Grow old along with me.
The rest is yet to be.
The last of life for which God made the first.
Goodbye to mates and friends.
Hello to (Christ!) Depends.
You only have rehearsed for being hearsed.

PETITION. THE RESIDENTS OF THE BELNORD APART-
MENT HOUSE DEMAND THE EXPULSION OF THOMAS J.

MURPHY FROM THE BUILDING AS SOON AS POSSIBLE. MANY OF US HAVE COMPLAINED OF MR. MURPHY'S PUBLIC DISPLAYS IN RECENT MONTHS. HIS LATE-NIGHT SINGING IN THE COURTYARD, IN INAPPRO-PRIATE DRESS AND IN AN INEBRIATED CONDITION. HIS CONTINUALLY LEAVING HIS FRONT DOOR OPEN, AS WELL AS HIS ATTEMPT TO BREAK INTO MRS. LIV-INGSTON'S APARTMENT. HIS CARELESSNESS IN HIS KITCHEN, LEADING TO A NEAR FIRE IN THE BUILDING. MOST RECENTLY, HIS ATTEMPT TO STEAL MR. BOTS-FORD'S VESPA AND THEN PUSHING IT TO THE GROUND, AWAKENING THE RESIDENTS. THESE DISTURBANCES HAVE PROMPTED THE OWNERS OF THE BUILDING TO ASK MR. MURPHY TO LEAVE, TO WHICH REQUEST MR. MURPHY HAS NOT RESPONDED. WE THE UNDERSIGNED SUPPORT THE OWNERS' EFFORTS IN THIS REGARD. ONCE SIGNED, THIS PETITION WILL BE PRESENTED TO THE BUILDING'S ATTORNEYS FOR IMMEDIATE ACTION.

    DANIEL A. PERACHIK

    SUPERINTENDENT

TELL ME WHAT I see, she says. I position her, as if she were posing for a portrait. Synge's Chair never looked lovelier, the rocks tinged with moss and orange-iron. Even the scraggy fields glow green. She is wearing an Irish sweater she bought herself for the trip, and with her hair blowing about in the cold sunshine, you never would know that she was not born and reared in my native land. In certain poses, at certain times, Oona would take my breath away. Sarah takes my breath away here. It has been a while since I felt a surge of happiness, or freedom for that matter. I clasp her by the shoulders, and kiss her for the first time, at long last. She kisses back. Enough of that for the time being, she says. Tell me what I see.

Directly in front of you, the rocks of Synge's Chair are mostly flat and arranged in a semicircle with a narrow opening to the right through which you entered, I tell her. The line of the Atlantic is narrow from this vantage point. You see a blue slash of water, as if an artist had moved his brush under the horizon with a lateral sweep of the hand. Above that, the sky is a mixture of blue and white, the white wispy and hazy, coquettish, vague. It stands out against the black rocks directly before you.

Ah, the rocks, she says. You love the rocks. I do, I say. One sits in Synge's Chair, I tell her, and automatically the eye goes to the sea and sky, skipping over the very sight that makes the sea and sky beautiful. The topmost rock looks like a hog's skull. The one to the left of it, a caveman's head with a protruding jaw. Both rocks rest on one that resembles a stubborn potentate with a white nose. He is wearing the two rocks above him as a headdress, perhaps a pair of turbans. To the left and right of him are two children rocks, leaning on their da. I see it, says Sarah.

In the crevices of the rocks lie secrets, I tell her. Notes and poems and fragments of thoughts people wrote a thousand years ago, rolled them into scrolls, and stuck them deep in the dark damp holes, too deep for us to reach. If we listen attentively, we can hear the messages buried in the holes. But they come out jumbled and incoherent, so rather than try to make out the words, we hear them all combined into a solemn piece of music. Monks' chants. I am trying to hear that music, says Sarah. But what more can I see? The sky is changing shape, I say. The white clouds swell in a pulse, and are larger and more pronounced. Do the rocks change as the sky changes? she asks. If you look long and hard, they do. Yes, I say. She says, I'll look long and hard.

What's to the left of me, Murph? Flat land sloping. Green, gray, white, and then the sea, I tell her. Now here, from this perspective, the line of the Atlantic appears much thicker than a brushstroke, and the blue is deeper, stronger, like a decision made and stuck to after much waffling. It is definite, the right decision. What has been decided? she asks. You'll have to ask the ocean, I tell her. Three white-walled cottages crop up where the green meets the gray. From here they look quite small, I say, like the toy houses provided with electric train sets. One has a tin roof, and a red door. The doors of the other two are black, and the roofs are thatch. If one peers closely, it appears that the white wall of the tin-roofed cottage has strands of silver and blue in it, like swimming herring, and pink flowers growing at the base. One of the flower heads is bowed in meditation. You can't see it from here, says Sarah. You're making that up. I am, I tell her. She smiles.

Inside the cottage with blue and silver fish in the walls, I go on, a couple sits reading in frayed chintz chairs. How old are the couple? she asks. He's seventy-two. She looks to be in her early, perhaps midthirties. Early, says Sarah. Definitely early. Anyone can see that. So, they are father and daughter? says Sarah, forcing her face into innocence. Let me look closer, I say. No. The way their bodies are angled toward each other, they appear to be lovers, or man and wife. The two being mutually exclusive? says Sarah. What are they reading? Can you make that out? I tell her, I can't see what the woman in her early thirties is reading (the Sarah smile), but the man has a book of Ben Jonson's poems. Wait. He's reading "His Excuse for Loving." Do you know it? Sarah shakes her head. The print is too small for me to read, but by a lucky coincidence, I know the poem by heart. That is lucky, says Sarah. What's the poem about? she asks. It's about the love of an old man for a much younger girl, I tell her. Never happens, she says. Recite it?

> Let it not your wonder move,
> Less your laughter, that I love.
> Though I now write fifty years,

I have had, and have, my peers;
Poets, though divine, are men,
Some have lov'd as old again.
And it is not always face,
Clothes, or fortune, gives the grace;
Or the feature, or the youth.
But the language and the truth.

She says nothing, but rather turns her head to the side. What's to the right of me, Murph? To the right of you, the land begins with boulders, then slopes down past the stiles to the sea that looks different yet again. Here the water is tinged with pink and gray, and appears less definite, though not wishy-washy. More like someone accustomed to ambiguity. On the shore, several seagulls stand tall and still, as if listening to instructions. They face east, every one of them. The grasses around them are yellow-green. The sky directly over them shows a gray funnel at the top. Are there more rocks on this side of me? she asks. No, I tell her. Here it is clear, save for a donkey about fifteen yards away, standing as still as the birds. His belly is a brownish gray, and his legs and face are white. He seems both drowsy and anxious. If you were my grandson, William, I'd tell you the donkey has wings, great golden wings. Does he have wings? asks Sarah. Yes, I say.

What else is there to see, Murph? Well—scanning the scene again—*there*. How did I miss that? Someone has created a tall stack of flat stones in the shape of a giant beehive. Really? she says. Yes, I tell her. I mean, *really*? she says. Yes. This is true. It's quite remarkable. Must be seven or eight feet high. And there are two sheep on either side of it, standing like royal guards. Why would someone build such a thing out here, asks Sarah, where no one will see it? I could make up something about man controlling nature, or art for art's sake, I tell her, but my guess is that whoever built the thing simply did it to see if it could be done. A beehive made of stones. Like a poem, says Sarah. Like a poem, I say. Was that all there was to the Ben Jonson poem? she asks. No, I tell her, it goes on.

> With the ardour and the passion,
> Gives the lover weight and fashion.
> If you then will read the story,
> First prepare you to be sorry
> That you never knew till now
> Either whom to love or how:
> But be glad, as soon with me,
> When you know that this is she
> Of whose beauty it was sung;
> She shall make the old man young,
> Keep the middle age at stay,
> And let nothing high decay,
> Till she be the reason why
> All the world for love may die.

She is small, silent, motionless in Synge's Chair. Is that everything? she says finally. Do I see everything there is to see? There are two more things, I tell her. Over the top of the rock pile behind you, you can make out the horns of a cow with a white head, and brown eyes staring. Horns, she says. How do you know it's not a bull? It's a cow, I tell her. You can tell by the size of the head. And if I were to go around to the other side of the rocks, there are other ways of telling a bull from a cow. And the second remaining thing I see? she says. That's me, I tell her. Me looking at you. Oh, she says. I always see you, Murph. I'll sleep with you tonight, I say. You'd better, she says.

HOW WILL I KNOW it's you at the door? she asks, because we have separate rooms across the hall from each other in the B and B, and Mrs. McGeary, our hag of a landlady, gave us the fish eye when we registered. I tell her I'll knock four times—two knocks followed by a pause followed by two more knocks. And I'll be as quiet as a mouse, I say, because if Mrs. McGeary senses any hanky-panky, the whole of greater Inishmaan will be giggling at us in the morning. Well, says Sarah, you might not make much noise with your four knocks, but the two of us may be making a ruckus after that. We may just have to live with the giggles.

To tell you the truth, I was wondering if I could get it

up even once after all this time, but the wondering evaporated at the sight of Sarah. I knocked my four knocks, and
she opened the door naked, her body spotlit by the light in
the hall. Murph? She laughed. This had better be you. I got
it up once, and I got it up twice, with a half hour's interval.
And after the second time, we lay in the cool sheets, with
the smell of turf around us, and her sweet head resting on
the white hairs of my chest. After a long silence, we said I
love you, at exactly the same time, as if each of us were dis-
closing a secret. And right after that, her cell phone made
the voice mail sound.

SOMEWHERE A CHILD CRIES tonight. A wailing, then a
whimper. Outside my window branches appear then disappear. The wind blows them into view, then takes them
away. If you pay attention, you can hear the air shrink in
the cold. Nowhere near the Atlantic, I can see it nonetheless, on two shores. It rears up and gallops from here
to Inishmaan and back. I can make out every wave and
whitecap. I can make out the lines in each whitecap, and
the tangles in the lines. Dr. Spector spoke of the end of
a life attended by a final lucidity. Is this final lucidity?
When I had the chance, I should have asked the doctor if
the term meant the last moment of lucidity, or lucidity at
last. I feel a surprising strength.

NASA says it has discovered 715 new planets with its

Kepler Space Telescope. With my naked eye I can detect
633. There is life on four of them. One is green. One is
secular. One is populated by sculptors. One, by gossips. As
for our terra firma, a frosty fog has obscured the particu-
lars. But just beside it, or above, or below (it seems continually to shift its position, like the branches) I see the
not at last, the world's not, and it is as clear as a bell, or a
raindrop—every petal booming and clanging. Thank you,
Professor Dodds. The final lucidity is the world's not. I
should tell someone. Whom should I tell? To whom should
I report my newfound clarity? I am Ella Fitzgerald singing
"All through the Night," pitch-perfect. So run my dreams.

Cold, cold. I should mind it more than I do, dressed
only in pajamas, and no shoes. I don't know. It feels balmy,
like Greece perhaps. Is this where vines grow out of the
planks of ships? I crave gaudier miracles. They dwell
here, somewhere, I am sure of it. I shall find them. We
shall find them. Together we shall oversee Máire and William, Sarah, too, and Arthur, and my homeless beauties,
the sullen carriage horses, even Jack, even (am I about to
say this?) Perachik—all those who need oversight from
our place of difference, our irrational world. Will I write
poems here? Less lyrical, I think. More like the old heroic
stuff created not because more heroes were in abundance
in the ancient then, but rather because poets felt the need
for heroes so urgently, they were compelled to bring them
to life.

But I also may do no poems in this place. Maybe there are no poems here. Maybe those who live here feel that poetry has had its day, the product of an elementary stage of evolution when the race was conscious of itself but little else. Maybe we are supposed to be the poems.

See here. A rose full of stars. Wells in the riverbanks. A keyhole in a badger. A sword swallower with bright blond hair and a love song stuck in his gullet. The painted windows of a church rattling in tune. Thatch. Turf. Uncertain loveliness. I walk warm paving stones, like ellipses, toward a Dionysian freedom disrupting the degrading monuments, the square this and the locked that, striding from the clinging snow into spring again. My birth lies in the raw silence of the day of the week beyond Sunday, the death beyond death, a cloven light. Lucid, pellucid. Final, eternal. When all that one has known or been withdraws, what then? Where am I standing, or not standing? A rustling from behind a pyramid of sedge. Darlin', is that you?

IS THAT YOU, Mr. Murphy? I think so, Mrs. Lewis, I barely say. She is standing with her husband in front of me near the fountain in the courtyard. I must have wandered here in my sleep. Oh, my dear man, she says. Let us walk with you back to your apartment. You just returned from Ireland. Didn't you? You must be jet-lagged. Yes, jet-lagged, I say. You've been very kind to me. Very good neighbors. I'll miss you both. Are you going somewhere, Mr. Murphy? says Mrs. Lewis. The petition, I tell them. I'm sure you saw it, even if you didn't sign it. They're tossing me out on my ear.

They stand there stunned, she with tears in her eyes. And I am moved that this lovely woman, whom I know only from the building, is crying for me. And she is, but not in the way I'm thinking. Don't you know, Mr. Murphy? she says, touching my arm. There wasn't a single signatory to that ridiculous petition. Not a one. Unless you count that wretched nosy parker, Perachik. And he won't be with us much longer, if the Tenants Committee has anything to say about it. No, no, no, dear Mr. Murphy. We tore down that petition the day after you left for Ireland, and all your friends and admirers in the Belnord got together, and agreed to tell you that, and to tell you why. Don't you know how we cherish you, Mr. Murphy? Why, man, says Mr. Lewis, you're our poet. You're our music. We'd kick out Perachik in a shot. But you? You're the music.

Speaking of which, it turned out, according to the Lewises, that no one had objected to my singing in the courtyard. They liked it. And no one gave a shit about the open doors, or about my trying to get in Mrs. Livingston's apartment, especially Mrs. Livingston. Botsford was tickled that I admired his Vespa so much I'd try to ride it. As for nearly setting my apartment on fire because of the eggs, Mr. Lewis said that half the tenants do that, and that he himself left his coffeemaker on last Labor Day weekend, and it burned a crater in the kitchen counter. Jones, Berman, and the DeBoks took up a petition insisting that I stay put. And Mrs. Ginnilli's book club has decided to dedicate the year to all my works, and voted that I must attend every one of their meetings as punishment, and explain myself. I am teary, and the Lewises are teary, and by the time we mount the steps and stagger to the elevator, the three of us look like drunken sailors err-lie in the morning.

I DON'T KNOW what else to tell you. The voice mail Sarah received from Jack heaved with remorse and contrition. He was full of shame, and full of sorrow, and he begged Sarah to take him back. He even quoted me (without attribution) from our chat in At Swim-Two-Birds, saying how smart and good a person Sarah is. I wasn't moved, and I don't think Sarah was either. But, as much as she loved me, she said, she would give him one more chance, or, as she put it, one more look. She had said she was cursed with feeling sorry for Jack, and so it seemed. I said nothing. Much as I loved her, what was there to say? One of the reasons I adored Sarah was her sense of honor and fair play. Who would I love after Oona but such a person?

On Aer Lingus back to New York, I told her I thought she was doing the right thing. The difference in our ages

was a cold fact. Even if I do have another twenty years
coming to me, when I finally go, she'll be in her fifties,
with no husband and nearly half a life spread out before
her like the Gobi Desert. Sarah answered that the trouble
was she was too old for me, and she had a point. But what
was real was real. The rocks.

And there was the matter of the prospect of my
incredible shrinking brain. And if it happens that my
bloody system does contain the e-4 time bomb, and
that my memory is on its way out, why on earth would I
want to hand this blessed girl one more disability? Her
response was like her. Everyone is disabled, she said.
Love exists for our disabilities. And if love were the only
thing to consider, she continued . . . But then her voice
trailed off, and she fell asleep on my shoulder for the rest
of the flight.

Máire and William are coming over in a few weeks,
so that's a good thing. I'd thought of visiting them when I
was in Ireland, but I wouldn't have wanted Sarah to travel
home alone. And my black Irish mood was blacker than
ever, so why expose Máire and William to that. I haven't
worked on Oona's poem in a while, or Greenberg's, but I'll
get there. I have a new book in mind, too. Only a title so
far. *Stone Harvest.* In the meantime, there'll be readings
here and there, and appearances where I'll play the public
man and yearn for home. Sounds corny, I know, but there's
nothing in a poet's life like doing poems. In the morning

stillness, my coffee, my chair, my legal pad, my mulling. For now, I pour myself a nightcap. *Sláinte.*

In bed on Inishmaan, I'd asked Sarah if she'd given any more thought to my question, What am I doing the rest of my life, and she sang, Spend it all with me. Naturally, that was before Jack's message. Yet she was right. What should one do with the rest of one's life? Spend it with Sarah. If you can't do that, shoot yourself. And if you won't do that, do whatever you did before the rest of your life. What you did in order to get to the rest of your life in one piece. You lived. So live. More noisily than ever. Court life. Woo the fucker. Sing it a love song. Belt it out at the top of your lungs. A pure restatement of the original theme. You never crash if you go full tilt. What is articulated strengthens itself. Sing it. In the courtyard, in the ashen sea, the muddied air, the bloodstained snow, the blackthorn bush, the damp straw, the field, the turf, the cold-eyed stars, and in the rocks, the rocks, the rocks. Sing it.

GOOD NIGHT. A bit of reading before sleep? Yeets? Too wiped. The soft hills of the coverlid. The sweeping tides of the sheets. I dive and tumble toward dreams, when something rattles the house. Two knocks followed by a pause followed by two more knocks. Have I told you about this?

ROGER ROSENBLATT is the author of six off-Broadway plays and eighteen books, including *Lapham Rising, Making Toast, Kayak Morning,* and *The Boy Detective.* He is the recipient of the 2015 Kenyon Review Award for Literary Achievement.